# BUCHANAN
# ON THE RUN

# BUCHANAN ON THE RUN

Jonas Ward

A FAWCETT GOLD MEDAL BOOK

Fawcett Publications, Inc., Greenwich, Conn.

*BUCHANAN ON THE RUN*

All characters in this book are fictional, and any resemblance to persons living or dead is purely coincidental.

Copyright © 1974 by Fawcett Publications, Inc.

Printed in the United States of America
May 1974

# BUCHANAN ON THE RUN

# Chapter 1

Tom Buchanan had never been happier. It was Thanksgiving, and the weather on El Camino Real was sunny and warm as it could be only in Southern California. Nightshade, the big black horse, played his little morning game, pirouetting and pretending to buck. Buchanan tilted back his sombrero to enjoy a cloudless sky.

Buchanan was six feet four in his stocking feet. He was a sandy man, with hair not quite red and freckles on his never-quite-bronzed fair skin. Scars marked his huge body, crisscrossing the muscular configuration. But there was always the hint of smile on his lips. He was a peaceable man on a peaceable errand this holiday season. His revolvers were tucked away in his saddlebag, and his rifle rode the boot, its stock encased in soft leather.

He rode toward the city known as Los Angeles, short for "El Pueblo de Nuestra Señora la Reina de los Angeles de la Porciuncula," which translated to "The Town of Our Lady the Queen of the Angels of Porciuncula," a mouthful not too difficult for a sandlapper from East

Texas. It was a town he had never before visited. While in the vicinity, he meant to see an old friend and enjoy the holiday.

He was enjoying El Camino Real, a broad road that had been inaugurated by Spanish explorers of long since, a natural highway that could be construed to run roughly between Los Angeles and San Francisco. There were rolling hills along each side of this valley, the San Fernando, extending to the Pacific Ocean not too many miles westward. Every prospect was pleasing.

There had been a significant lack of violence in California for quite some time. It had been weeks since Buchanan had been a party to or even a witness of anything of excitement. He expected no more at the hacienda of Don Pedro O'Brien, which should be close by, he reckoned. And if there was anything in the world that Tom Buchanan loved, it was peace and quiet.

There had been too many times when events had interfered with his enjoyment of life. There had been involvements in which the sounds of shot and the whirl of fists and clubs had found him an unwilling participant in melees not of his choosing. He bore the scars. Thus far, on this trip south, he had been most fortunate.

It happened that he was traveling toward a scene of minor violence, but in this he had a passive part. His long-time friend, the black prizefighter Coco Bean, was to meet another battler named Chino Cruz in Los Angeles. Buchanan hoped to do no more than bet a considerable sum on Coco.

Of the result he had no doubts. Coco was, in his opinion, the greatest heavyweight fighter in the world. In fact, Coco was in Coco's opinion the greatest fighter in the world. For some time, he had been attempting to get Buchanan to prove the point by crossing fists with him. It was a question Buchanan had no intention of settling. He had been doing all he could to avoid the meeting. He could see no advantage in winning—he didn't really care either way, and Coco might suffer a blow to his professional pride if Buchanan landed the first punch.

He was satisfied to bet against this Chino Cruz, whoever he might be. He wanted to allow himself further leisure to smell the blossoms, bask in the sunshine, and pursue the peaceful life. He had roamed the Western frontier since he had been orphaned in his teens, taking adventure as it came, enjoying each changing season, and appreciating the ineffable beauty of the West. Today, birds sang in live oaks lining the California highway, small animals darted in the brush, and little clouds flirted high in the blue sky. Buchanan drew a deep, contented breath into his forty-four-inch chest.

The sun hung high overhead when Nightshade swung to the right, whinnying, a sign of thirst. Buchanan allowed him his head, knowing he had scented out a water hole. There was a small stream running through heavy undergrowth, and he swung down, loosening the girth and removing the bit so that the big black horse might drink at his ease.

A jay darted, scolding. Buchanan laughed at the sharp-eyed, feisty bird and knelt to cup his hands into the water somewhat upstream from Nightshade. He washed the dust from his hands and face and dried them on the kerchief about his neck, whistling a little tune. He was looking forward to a visit with Don Pedro, whom he had known as plain Peter O'Brien in other, wilder days.

There was bit of the rascal in Peter, who was reputedly rich now on his hacienda. His cattle and his orange and walnut groves were abounding. He had always been a gambler for high stakes, and he had never been to careful about the means to gain his end. But he was warm and loyal to his friends, and he was always good for a bit of fun. Buchanan was no great whiskey-drinker, but he liked to have a few with Peter O'Brien on occasion, and this was Thanksgiving, a holiday.

He tightened the girth and restored the bit to the Nightshade's tender-tough mouth. He saw to his saddle-bags, where his belt and six-gun were, as usual, wrapped and out of sight. He tightened the rifle in its scabbard, feeling grateful for the peace of the countryside.

It was then that he heard voices. From long experience on the frontier, he stood silently in the little glade beside the stream, realizing that he was concealed by the brush and by an enormous oak tree.

A high, whining voice asked, "What time you got, Silk?"

"I jist toldja, dummy." The second voice was hoarse and rasping. "Whattsa matter, you scared or somethin'?"

"Damn people comin' and goin' on the road, is all. Nemmine me. You just be sure you get the right one."

"You just make sure you know what's doin', Dugan."

Something told Buchanan that what was doing was wrong. He slid the rifle from the saddle and admonished Nightshade to silence with a touch on the horse's velvet nose. He padded toward the voices, making no sound. All the birds and insects and little beasts had become silent. He crept close to another thick growth of under-brush that concealed the two men.

Now there was the sound of harness, a carriage coming down the road toward the west, in the direction from which Buchanan had been traveling. The road was level and the carriage was proceeding at a normal speed.

The two men began to work their way through the brush. Buchanan followed in their wake. His progress went unheard in the noise they were making. They suddenly stopped, and Buchanan knelt, peering. He saw that they had reached a vantage point commanding the road.

One was tall and slim and wore rough garments, not range clothing but more like store-bought working clothes.

The other was shorter and stouter and wore, surprisingly, the black coat and striped pants of the gambler. Each had masked himself with a big white-and-blue checkered kerchief, the kind sold in city stores, not the cowboy's pañuelo like the one Buchanan wore.

The high voice said, "It's them, Silk. Now stay the hell out of the way, you hear?" This was Dugan, the heavy-set man, the gambler. He had a rifle in his hands.

The other said, "I got to stop 'em, don't I? So make damn sure of your shot."

"You do your job. I'll do mine."

"You better had."

"Aw, go on the hell out there."

"I'm a-goin'."

The man named Silk stepped out onto the shoulder of El Camino Real. He held a nickel-plated .38 revolver in each hand—city weapons. The other man, Dugan, who remained in the brush, was handling a carbine rather than a rifle—army issue, Buchanan thought. These were city people, all right, out to commit a murder. The carriage drew nearer. There were two passengers, and Buchanan had time to see that one was a female.

Then he was standing, his rifle cradled, saying loudly, "Just take it easy there. Don't make a move."

The man at the edge of the road froze, dropping his revolvers. The other hesitated. Buchanan pulled the trigger, and a bullet sailed past the ear of the other man, who got rid of the carbine in a hurry.

The carriage drew abreast. Peter O'Brien was driving. A lady was at his side. Buchanan called out, "Peter! It's me, Tom Buchanan! Hold up."

There was the sound of a shot. It came from the other side of the road. O'Brien bent low and slapped reins on a matched pair of gray ponies. They took off like greyhounds.

Another bullet sang its little song, nicking the brim of

Buchanan's hat. On its heels came another, which almost scratched his throat. Belatedly, he flung himself back into the brush and made a circular path back toward Nightshade.

Bullets rained after him as the two he had scouted regained their weapons and joined the attack with the unseen partner from the other side of the road, the man on whom Buchanan had not reckoned.

"Cross fire," he muttered to Nightshade as he mounted. "They were takin' no chances. They wanted O'Brien—or the woman—real bad. Sent three to do one man's job."

He rode back to the road. There was no sight nor sound of the three bushwhackers. Either they had gone back toward Los Angeles, or they were pursuing the carriage. Buchanan had no choice. He turned Nightshade westward along the road in the path of the carriage, the lady, and O'Brien. He held the rein in his left hand and the rifle in his right, leaning, searching the horizon.

The carriage had slackened pace and was pulling off the road. Buchanan rode up, descended, and dropped the muzzle of the rifle into the scabbard. Nightshade remained at the rear of the carriage.

O'Brien said, "Figured it was you, back there. These damn highwaymen have been gettin' wild lately."

"Uh-huh," said Buchanan. He was looking at the young lady. Her hair was dark as night, and she had widespaced, almost oriental eyes and a reckless slash of a scarlet mouth. She was unsmiling, her gaze searching Buchanan with more than casual interest. There seemed to be no fear in her, merely curiosity and controlled excitement. She wore a man's shirt open at the neck, a divided skirt, and dusty boots, but about her was a dramatic quality that Buchanan recognized. She was a lady who could cause trouble, tall, beautifully formed, vital.

"We come lookin' for you to make sure you'd find the ranch," Peter was saying, controlling his voice with effort.

"Sure never expected to be held up on El Camino Real."

"Yeah," said Buchanan. "How you been besides that?"

Peter O'Brien batted his eyes. He was a florid, balding man of medium height. He was dressed in corduroy, with high-laced boots and a flat, wide-brimmed hat. Buchanan knew that O'Brien was scared, but he was no less dangerous in his fear. He was a man who fought back when sweating it out. There was a certain quality to O'Brien, even in his sometime rascality.

"Fine . . . fine. You get a good look at those people back there?"

"Fair. Two city boys. One I didn't see chased me with some pretty good shootin', which let 'em all get away."

"Three of 'em?" O'Brien squinted, nodding to himself. "Yeah. That'd be Big Jim's people, all right."

The girl said, "Excuse me, Peter. May I be introduced?"

"Oh! Hey, yeah." O'Brien shrugged himself together. "Tom, this here is Tim's widow. Jenny O'Brien."

Buchanan removed his Stetson. "Heard about Tim. Sorry, Mrs. O'Brien."

"Pleased to meet you, Tom Buchanan." Her voice was full, deep, even stagy, as though she had worked on it. "Shouldn't we get about Thanksgiving and forget the—er—holdup men? Peter? Shouldn't we, really?"

"Uh . . . sure."

"What about those dudes up yonder?" asked Buchanan. "You think they gave up that easy?"

"We'll go the back way," said O'Brien. "There's an old trail through the groves."

Buchanan said, "Lead on. I'll just keep the rifle handy."

"Oh, they wouldn't know . . ." O'Brien broke off, turn-the team up the road.

Buchanan mounted Nightshade and followed closely, keeping his eye peeled for an ambush. His mind was working over several moot points.

First, despite O'Brien's assertion, the bushwhackers

were not holdup men. They were killers out to perform an assassination. There was absolutely no doubt about this. Secondly, O'Brien and the woman knew this was true, despite the talk about holdup men on the highway leading to Los Angeles.

Then there was the late Tim O'Brien, younger brother of Peter, a youth Buchanan had never favored. Many times in the past, it had been Tim who had inaugurated sneaky deals in which Peter was involved. A couple of times, Buchanan had been the one to ride to the rescue. Now he remembered that Tim had gone East, to New York, from whence he had returned with his bride.

The couple had settled on Peter's hacienda, which had begun to prosper a couple of years before. Peter had won it in a poker game, hired knowledgeable Mexican help, and settled down to some hard work. All this had come to Buchanan's ears, in one way or another. News ran rampant on the Western frontier; it was not always correct, but it was always plentiful.

And then Tim had been killed in Los Angeles under mysterious circumstances. The city had just been beginning to grow, with the arrival of the Southern Pacific Railroad. Tim had mixed into politics in some way or another, had gone against the top man, and had lost. He had shouted foul—which was undoubtedly true—and someone had carved him up in a dark alley on a summer night in this same year.

His widow, Buchanan thought, was not wearing black, neither literally nor metaphorically. Since Tim had been a handsome, laughing young villain, this might or might not be odd behavior. It was something to occupy Buchanan's mind.

His senses were otherwise assailed. The carriage proceeded between wide-spaced rows of trees, first gnarled walnut trees and then serried orange trees that were bearing fruit even in November. The winter crop, Buchanan thought. He had heard tales of the odd climate of Southern California. Lotus land, people said. Some avoided it, because they said it was sinful, against all nature. There was never any snow and almost no frost. This, besides all else, was unhealthy, they claimed.

There were cattle on the rolling hills to the north, fat and sleek cattle. It might be contrary to nature, but it all looked mighty prosperous, Buchanan decided. There might come a day when he would finally settle down and quit his wandering. From now on, this country would ever be in his mind. The temperature was many degrees warmer here among the trees than back on El Camino Real. Amazing country, indeed. Even Nightshade snorted, wagging his head and swishing his tail as though the prospect pleased him.

Finally, the house came within sight. The house was familiar to Buchanan. It was a low, one-storied house of lodge-pole design, constructed of adobe brick made by first-class artisans. There was a whitewashed fence enclosing a large patio. The stable for the horses was convenient but not too close. Care and thought had gone into the building of the place. Buchanan remembered that Peter had won it from an aging California hidalgo who had too much faith in an ace-high flush. The house had been run-down, but the original owner, now long forgotten, had had good sense and good taste. Peter had done his best to restore its soft, informal, welcoming aspect.

A brown-faced boy came to attend the horses. A lean, leathery majordomo spoke in rapid Spanish with O'Brien, shook his head, and then strode off to relay orders to the vaqueros or other hired hands. It seemed only reasonable that a guard should be set against the three would-be killers.

A houseboy came to take Buchanan's saddlebags. The woman descended from the carriage, and he saw she was taller than O'Brien. She was long-legged and graceful, catlike. She murmured something meant to be polite and slithered off down a corridor.

O'Brien said, "She ain't happy here."

"Is that it?" Buchanan waited.

"Wants to go back to New York. She was on the stage or somethin'. Never did get it straight. Tim—you know how he was. She don't talk to me much."

"Why don't she go back there?"

"Cash," said O'Brien. "Don't look surprised. "I put everything back into this place. Then I tried Big Jim's game. Busted me for cash. Fact is, he's got a mortgage."

"And wants to kill you?"

O'Brien said, "Let's have a drink." He led the way into a dining roof filled with heavy Spanish furniture. The odor of cooking came from the kitchen in the rear. "Turkey and all the trimmin's. We eat good, don't cost nothin'. If we get one good crop, sell some beef, I'll be okay. Cucamongo knows that."

"Cucamongo? Why, that's the fella promotin' the fight between Coco and Chino Cruz."

"Sure he is. He owns half of Los Angeles and just about controls the other half. Didn't you know that?"

"Never paid any heed," said Buchanan. "Never had business in the town."

"It's growed." O'Brien led the way out into the patio. A Mexican woman appeared with a pitcher of water and glasses. They sat at a table of native redwood, and O'Brien poured with a heavy hand.

Buchanan added a quantity of water and watched his friend drink four ounces straight. "So you got troubles?"

"Tim was buckin' Big Jim when he got his," said O'Brien. "But there's no proof. Jenny tried to learn somethin' and got plenty scared. Big Jim's still after her. Not to kill her, neither."

"I see."

"He even offered to marry her."

"Now that's mighty big of him. This fella sounds right interestin'," said Buchanan. "'Course those three jaspers were his men out there tryin' to kill you."

"Yes, and they would've got in a shot if I'd been alone," said O'Brien. "They'd of let you alone and got me. They had to be careful not to get Jenny instead."

"Uh-huh," Buchanan said. "Still, I knew they weren't road agents. I heard two of 'em talkin'."

"Yeah . . . well." O'Brien drank, poured again. "Always thought I was pretty slick. Big Jim's twice as tricky and smart. He'll get me sooner or later. If Jenny leaves, it'll be sooner."

"You and Jenny pretty close, are you?"

"Nope." O'Brien hit the whiskey. "Not that I ain't tried. After Tim went, she looked mighty good to me. She's just got this one thing, goin' back to New York. Actin' on the stage."

"Too much dirt and noise," Buchanan said. "Can't take a deep breath of good air."

"I remember, you was back there with Luke Short."

"Few years ago," Buchanan said. "Never seen so many people in one place."

The throaty voice said behind him, "But that's what makes it great, Mr. Buchanan. It's big and vital, and the people attend the theater and are generous with their applause. That's what makes it the best city in the country."

He got up, bowing. She wore a red velvet gown that was exceedingly tight in the bust and across the hips. It was cut low, the skirt flaring out to give freedom to the long legs. Her hair was pulled back, and she wore a red rose behind one ear. He had indeed seen ladies on the stage who had been similarly attired—and in rather disreputable houses.

The Mexican woman brought in a carafe of red wine and a small goblet. Beaming, she poured for Jenny

O'Brien, who seated herself with a swirl of red-velvet skirt.

Buchanan said, "Everyone to his own taste, as the old lady said when she kissed the cow."

"The cow? How odd!" Jenny O'Brien sipped her wine.

O'Brien poured heavily into his glass. "Aw, come off it, Jenny. You're not goin' to con Buchanan out of train fare. He's dry behind the ears, believe me."

Into the embarrassment Buchanan said gallantly, "Let the lady try, Peter, let her try. She's pretty enough to make a go of it."

Unperturbed, the lady said, "Thank you, Mr. Buchanan. You sound like a real New Yorker."

"Bullfeathers," said O'Brien. "I'm gonna wash up. Anything you want—exceptin' cash—just yell, Tom. Or ask Jenny, she's been here long enough to know the ropes."

He went from the room, carrying his whiskey glass a trifle unsteadily. The lady stared after him. Buchanan watered another whisky.

She hitched her chair closer to the table, and the lace mantilla fell from her shoulders. She was rounded, smooth, and slightly tanned from the California sun. She swallowed the wine and refilled her glass.

She said, "He's right, I'd do anything for the train fare back East."

"Sounds kinda drastic," Buchanan observed, squinting at her.

"Well . . . almost anything." She flushed. "Jim Cucamongo offered me a job in his theater and I turned it down."

"He owns a theater?"

"And a hotel and a bank—which is how he got the mortgage on this place. And a couple of judges and several policemen and a crooked prosecutor and a defense lawyer who's a cousin to the prosecutor," she said.

"You mean nobody else in Los Angeles owns anything?"

"If he does, he owes Big Jim a favor. Or he's so busy he doesn't pay attention. Oh, they're a few citizens, a Mexican-American or two, there's always somebody."

"Even against Boss Tweed in New York," said Buchanan. "I heard about 'em but never met one."

"Yes, Boss Tweed." Her voice had altered, becoming natural. It was deep and pleasing when she did not use the stagy accent she had earlier assumed.

"I got a mighty good friend mixed up with Cucamongo," Buchanan said. "Coco Bean."

"He hasn't a chance," she said. "They'll finish him off. They have all the cards."

Buchanan thought for a moment, tasting the watered whiskey. Then he said, "So happens I'm carryin' some money. It don't mean much to me, money. Buys a little time to rest, look around, be with friends."

"Yes?" she said breathlessly.

"You seem to know a heap about Cucamongo and Los Angeles."

"My husband was killed there!"

"Yeah. Your husband. I knew him . . . but never mind that."

"I do mind it. I learned about him before he died."

"Uh-huh," said Buchanan. "What I'm gettin' at is the situation with Coco. I'll be goin' in, makin' bets, watchin' over him. Now, if someone was to lend a hand, give us some backin' with knowledge of the setup, I'd be more'n willing to pay off in cash. 'Specially if we win the fight."

"You can't win," she said in despair. "There's nothing I can do. There are too many of them. Big Jim's too clever."

"That's what Peter said, and I never heard him admit anybody was slicker then him. It don't seem possible."

She said, "Big Jim outsmarted Tim, then Peter. I know all about that. I saw it happen."

"You didn't see through the schemin'?"

"No," she said honestly, meeting his gaze. "I was a dancer, a singer, an actress when I was a young girl. I don't claim to have brains—only talent. That's why I want to go where people recognize what I can do. Can you blame me?"

"Like I said," Buchanan lifted a shoulder. She was a strange woman, a woman of shifting moods. "None of my business, is it? Look, tell me about Peter. Is he plumb scared of Cucamongo?"

She relaxed, seemingly indifferent. "I don't know. Baffled, maybe. He was always a better fighter than Tim."

"You think Cucamongo wants him dead so he can take over the ranch?"

"And me."

Buchanan shook his head. "It don't add up good. Murder, that's a bad thing, and when you hire killers you always got trouble. They talk."

She sipped at the wine. "Are you saying that Big Jim is not as clever as we think?"

"That remains to be seen." Buchanan was getting the impression that she was not really interested in anything that did not directly concern her and her return to imagined fame and fortune in New York.

Heels clicked on the tile floor, and Peter O'Brien returned to the dining room. His cheeks were spotted pink, and he was smiling expansively. Following him were two guitar-players and a smiling Mexican with maracas. They began strumming and clicking the old chestnut Buchanan had heard south of the border so often, *La Paloma*.

O'Brien had unquestionably been at another bottle. He had changed to velveteen pants, a full, white blouse, and a bolero jacket. He was now Don Pedro of the hacienda. The Mexican woman was bowing and smiling in the background, announcing that the dinner was ready.

"Drink up," O'Brien cried. "Eat, drink, and be merry.

Songs and dancin', that's the ticket. Forget your troubles!"

From the kitchen came brown-faced, smiling people bearing platters of turkey, mashed potatoes, and all the trimmings. Peter did a clumsy dance step.

The woman arose, the wine glass in her hand. Her figure swayed as though in a breeze, and her feet described intricate figures. The skirt twirled, revealing beautifully formed ankles and silken calves. She spun in a tarantella of her own concoction, Buchanan thought. It was not a Spanish dance, but something both slower and faster. Her concentration was tremendous; she had forgotten the hacienda, the people, all but the music. She was bemused, lost in the convolutions of her dance. She still held the wine, never spilling a drop. She was as lovely as a wood sprite.

Peter had stopped moving and was softly clapping his hands in rhythm. A look at his eyes divulged that he had not been speaking idly when he had said he wanted the widow of his brother. Buchanan sat with his watered drink, his mind again turning to Coco Bean and Los Angeles and the dangers related by Peter and Jenny.

The music stopped, and they repaired to the table, which was now groaning with victuals. Buchanan ate as only he could when he was hungry—steadily, without fanfare, putting away an enormous quantity.

The music resumed, and the wine and whiskey flowed. Particularly potent was a California brandy, distilled by monks in the northern section of the state. Buchanan relaxed; the woman recommenced dancing, Peter O'Brien snapped his fingers, and the night wore on. It was good at last to retire to a comfortable bed in a room at the rear of the house where the Mexican woman did everything but tuck him in. Buchanan slept like a log. . . .

He awakened in the morning with the sun streaming in the window. The taste in his mouth was like the inside of a leather gauntlet. He staggered to the water basin and washed himself from head to toe. There were heavy towels and scented soap—Peter O'Brien lived well despite his lack of cash.

He dressed for the road and neatly packed his saddle-bags. Remembering the violence of yesterday, he placed the cartridge belt and Colt on top, where they would be convenient.

He plodded out to the kitchen, his head a bit cloudy. The Mexican woman handed him a steaming cup of coffee. She was not smiling this morning.

"Don Pedro?" Buchanan asked.

"Gone."

"Gone?" Buchanan couldn't believe it. O'Brien had been drunker than that last night, he must be sleeping it off.

"He no sleep here," said the woman. She was plainly worried. "She talk to him, he go."

"They went last night?" Ideas began to form in Buchanan's head.

"Last night," the woman nodded. She did not approve.

"To Los Angeles?"

"Si, señor. You go Los Angeles?" She gave the name of the town the soft Spanish inflection.

"Yes. Right now."

She brightened. "You see them."

"Most likely," he assented.

"You eat now." She turned toward the stove. She still had not smiled. There was fear at the O'Brien hacienda, all right.

Buchanan went outdoors to see to the needs of Nightshade. The Mexican stableboy also was gloomy, uncertain. The carriage and the mixed grays were missing.

Buchanan went back and ate bacon and eggs. Jenny O'Brien had undoubtedly prevailed upon Peter when he was high and full of whisky courage. Perhaps it was Buchanan's fault, perhaps his offer of train fare if she could aid Coco Bean had been her inspiration. In any case, he had to make tracks. The time of peace and quiet was ended.

# Chapter 2

"The Town Of Our Lady Queen of Angels of Porciuncula" was founded September 4, 1781, by Don Felipe de Never, Governor of California, which was then a province of Mexico. He led the customary troop of soldiers—and eleven families—north from their homes. Many of these original settlers were unwilling Negroes and Indians, some from the mission at San Gabriel. The scheme was to work farms, orchards, vineyards, taking advantage of the wondrous climate. Seedlings from Spain and slips from Mexico were provided. The soil seemed fairly fertile, despite a puzzling deposit of sand and clay in crisscross sections.

Each of the original families was given a lot to fertilize and a home-site facing the Plaza, a large square that formed the center of community life. By 1800, the settlement contained all of seventy families, who dwelt in adobe cabins and engaged chiefly in raising grain and cattle.

Nothing happened of significance for another seventy-six years. Then the Southern Pacific pushed its rail-head toward the sea, for the time being getting no further than

Los Angeles. The bay was miles distant at San Pedro, another sleepy settlement only occasionally active, since few profitable goods were shipped to the area. But when Buchanan rode in through the narrow, muddy streets there was plenty of action.

Building was going on in every direction. There were the theater and the Coliseum, owned by Jim Cucamongo. There were two hotels, the old one in the Plaza and a new one owned by Big Jim Cucamongo. There were houses along Alvarado Street and new ones going up every day. There were people of all races and colors, buzzing here and there, busily building a city out of a mud town.

There was a new, clean stable behind the Coliseum Hotel. Cucamongo evidently got a kick out of the hostelry's grandiose Roman name. Buchanan spoke to the Mexican attendant, bribed him with a silver dollar, took his saddlebags and his soogans, and went around to the lobby.

The desk clerk shoved a register forward with a limp, negligent wrist. Buchanan removed the pen from a rack, dipped it into the horn, and wrote his name in a large, legible hand. The clerk glanced at him, reached for a key, then paused and showed his bad teeth in a smile.

"Mr. Buchanan. Yes. You're expected." He switched to a different room-key and touched a small, tinkly handbell. When he moved, the butt of a small handgun was visible beneath his armpit. He had narrow eyes, now bland and blank. "My name's Chilton. Anything you need, just ask for me."

"Mighty fine of you," Buchanan said. "The man I'd like to see is Coco Bean. You know?"

"Indeed. You're his manager."

Buchanan had never been Coco's manager, but it did not seem the moment to make this clear. "Uh-huh. If I can just stow my gear first. Then get to see him."

"Certainly, Mr. Buchanan." A Mexican youth wearing

a red jacket appeared. He was a small young man with a wide smile. He bobbed his head, took the key from the clerk, and reached for Buchanan's saddlebags. Chilton went on, "Room 222. A bath down the hall. Hot water can be arranged. The door is marked 'for men only,' you can't miss it."

"Hope you got one for the ladies, too," said Buchanan. "Not that I don't prefer to bathe alone."

The main impression given by the hotel was one of newness. It was also big. The lobby floor was terrazo, made with a local stone. There were potted palms and rubber plants and a lot of glistening gilt paint. But unlike the San Francisco hotels known to Buchanan, it had no elevator. In fact, it all seemed a bit garish, even shoddy. The bellboy led the way up broad stairs. Buchanan cradled his rifle and wondered what was behind the rather sissified desk clerk who wore an underarm holster complete with weapon.

The room was large, but the ceiling was a bit too low. The window looked down upon a half-paved street. Across the way was a half-finished frame building that seemed to have stopped at the third story, after having lost the ambition to grow higher. The bed was clean and ample. There was a closet, a bureau, and two chairs, one upholstered in a coarse fabric, the other rawhide-hard. A commode held pitcher and washbasin. There was a Mexican rug on the floor. It was all comfortable and new, but not quite . . . opulent. He wondered how much he was paying per day.

He fished in his pocket for a silver four-bit piece and flipped it to the young man. "Your name?" he asked in Spanish.

"Tomás." The boy was polite but wary.

"Is Coco Bean staying here?"

"No, señor." Tomás was shocked. "He is black."

"Uh-huh. Well, where can I find him?"

"He trains at the theater. There is a charge for admission. He stays with a black family."

"Would he be trainin' about now?"

"Sí, señor. For the money, you see?"

"Oh, sure. I see. Big Jim Cucamongo collects the money."

"But, of course." Tomás did not smile.

"Tell me, sonny. You know two men called Silk and Dugan?"

Tomás's eyes glazed over. "No, señor, I know them not."

"But you know who they are?"

Tomás shook his head, his mouth tight. "It is better we do not speak of these men, señor. Your pardon."

He was gone out the door before there could be another question. Yet the boy had not altered his tone. His last look at Buchanan had been lingering, wondering. Buchanan filed that glance in the back of his mind.

He poured water into the basin. Remembering the bath, he found towels and went down the hall. The room was accessible through the use of his room key. He found it empty, and he availed himself of tepid water and a decent soap. He returned to his room, donned clean clothing, and sat for a moment, thinking about Peter O'Brien and the woman and Coco Bean and the bushwhackers and what he had learned secondhand about Big Jim Cucamongo. It did not add up to a peaceable future. He sighed and went back downstairs to the garish lobby.

He now noticed that there was a barroom beyond the desk. He entered and found it to be another large room with a long polished mahogany bar, a back mirror, the customary painting of a near-nude lady, and chandeliers arranged to favor a roulette wheel and a poker table. The nearest bartender smiled at him with upraised brows. Suddenly he scowled. He was a scar-faced man with a walrus mustache.

"Buchanan, is that you?"

"Well, howdy, Durand," Buchanan said. "Outa the pen, are you?"

"Uh-huh." Durand put a bottle of high-priced whiskey on the bar and slid a four-ounce shot glass before Buchanan. "Water on the side, ain't it?"

"You have a good memory." Buchanan put a dollar on the bar and watched it being swept away under a wide palm.

"You put me inna hospital for a month." He touched the scar on his cheek. "I don't forget people like you."

"Don't forget you were dealin' from the bottom. And you did pull that hidey gun. Lemme see, was that in Dodge or Abilene?"

"It was in Ogallala, and you know it good. And I pulled the gun on that damn little Luke Short, not you."

"But Luke's my friend," Buchanan said gently. "Further and more, you also forget how quick he is. Had I not busted you, he might've shot you dead."

"Yeah, well . . ." Durand tried to grin. "I don't forget. But I don't hold no grudges. Big Jim taught me that."

Buchanan finished his drink, poured again, and produced another coin to cover his surprise. "Big Jim Cucamongo?"

"Who else would hire a man fresh outa the pen and trust him behind the bar?" Durand was in earnest. "You ask anybody around here about Big Jim. He's the finest man in California. He'll be governor of this here state some day."

"You don't say."

"I do say. He about owns this town right now on account of his good deeds and all."

"Well, you see, I haven't ever been here before. I wouldn't know about such things," Buchanan said.

"You manage the nigger fighter," said Durand. "You oughta know somethin' about Big Jim."

"Been busy with other matters," Buchanan said. "Now, about the betting. How does that go?"

"This here's the place for action," said Durand. "Any amount, we can handle it. You want to bet on your nigger?"

Buchanan sighed, finishing his second whisky. "That's the second time."

"The second time what?"

"The second time you referred to Coco Bean as my 'nigger,' " said Buchanan.

"Well, he is, ain't he?"

"He's got a name. Coco Bean. And I got a feelin' against the word 'nigger.' Understand?"

"Now, wait a minute, Buchanan . . ."

"Bein' one of Big Jim's men and all, not holdin' grudges, you got to have understandin'. Coco Bean. Champion."

Durand clutched hard at the edge of the bar, and then one hand went instinctively to the scar on his face. "Uh . . . yeah. See whatcha mean. Yeah. Coco Bean. Champ. Okay, Buchanan."

"Thanks. Be seein' you around, Durand."

He started for the street exit. Then he became aware of being watched. He saw Tomás behind a large rubber plant. The young man was grinning. Buchanan paused and spoke without looking at him.

"Don't cotton to Mr. Durand, do you, amigo?"

"No, señor."

"Shows you got good sense. Might keep your eyes and ears open and remember what you hear. Could be worth some dinero."

"You could get into trouble, señor. Bad trouble."

"You mean Big Jim ain't a real good man? Durand says he is."

"He is a very big man. He owns everything around here." Tomás spoke in rapid English. "He pretends. Many people are enchanted with him. Sometimes he gives to the poor—food, clothing."

"I'll just have to meet up with this man."

"Yes. You are a very big man also. It will be—of great interest when you meet." Tomás lost his smile. "Other men have tried, good men."

"Tried what?"

"To overcome the greed of Cucamongo," said Tomás.

The bell at the desk tinkled. Tomás detoured away from the potted tree, and Buchanan sauntered out into the street. Wagons came and went in the dust, and people strolled as though they were in no great hurry, although destinations were in their minds. It was a nice, leisurely pace, and the November sun was warm and pleasant. Buchanan thought that perhaps Los Angeles might be a good place to live.

He observed the people with interest. There were members of every nationality that had made its home in the Southwest. A fairly large proportion were Chinese. He moved among them, towering above them. He drew quick glances from male and female alike as he turned the corner at the south side of the hotel.

The theater was a barnlike building. It was dwarfed by the hotel, but it was still a large enough palace of entertainment by frontier standards. There was an alley, closed to vehicular traffic, between the two edifices. Buchanan strolled in. He knew that this was the time to study the terrain, so that he would be ready for any circumstance. Each of the buildings had a back door; the two doors were precisely opposite one another. Beyond the theater was another, even narrower, alley, which he followed to the street.

He turned left and lingered beneath the marquee of the theater. There were signs announcing CHAMPIONSHIP EXHIBITION, CHINO CRUZ AND COCO BEAN TRAIN HERE. Admission 50c.

There were loungers, the sort who turned up for every boxing exhibition, and a single uniformed policeman wearing a large nickel-plated badge and a holstered .38 caliber revolver, a truly tough-looking individual. All stared at Buchanan, measuring his size and style.

There were voices from without. One of them was high and shrill, the other throaty. Buchanan recognized them at once. They belonged to two of the bushwhackers he had last heard along El Camino Real on the road to O'Brien's hacienda. He turned and faced them, studying them. They were medium-sized, as he remembered, and undistinguishable in appearance.

The third man, however, was of another stamp. He was tall, lean, and hairless. He had eyes that seemed to see everything, darting here and there, never still. His pale hands had long, spatulate fingers that were, like his eyes, seldom in repose.

The fourth member of the group was as tall as Buchanan, and heavier. His belly bulged beneath a checkered vest, across which was draped a gold chain. Emblems dangled from the chain, proclaiming him to be a member of the Foresters, the Eagles, and the Masonic Order. A diamond flashed on the third finger of his left hand. His face was round and cherubic. He smiled to show teeth capped with silver. Men stirred at sight of him, grinning, almost applauding, and seeking his notice. The ticket-taker, a ruffian in a sweater with a rolled neck, did everything but genuflect.

The three followers of the big man all wore badges.

The tall, lean man's eyes slid sideways, his hands fluttered as he whispered in the ear of the fat leader. The group came around on an oblique angle, walking easily toward Buchanan. They were, in various degrees, registering pleasure. It was a sight to behold, Buchanan thought, one he could never forget.

They stopped with military precision, flanking Buchanan. The fat man beamed at him, offering his hand, and saying cordially, "You just got to be Tom Buchanan. Heard all about you. From lots of people. Your man Coco will be right glad to see you, believe me. Welcome to Los Angeles, the fastest growing town in the entire West!"

Buchanan accepted the hand, which was cool and firm. "Big Jim Cucamongo, I take it."

"You take it right on the dot, sir," said the fat man. "Want you to meet Sheriff Deputy Hatfield and his men, Silk Wilks, the thin fellow there, and Bert Dugan."

"Uh-huh," said Buchanan, nodding. He retrieved his right hand and leaned back against the wall. He was not, of course, wearing his gunbelt, and never had he felt so naked without it. The grimaces on the faces of the three men with badges were a mockery. They would have loved to kill him on the spot. He was particularly aware of Hatfield's furtive eyes. The man removed his hat. He was completely bald.

Buchanan said, "Hatfield . . . Uh-huh. I mind you now, Hatfield. The Vandermeer case. Texas, about seven years ago. You were with the Pinkertons."

The pale face flushed. Hatfield's voice was husky, grating. "I was framed."

"So you said." It had been a murder case, and the Pinkertons had sent their best bloodhound to ferret out the killer. Hatfield had failed, and rumor persisted that he had taken a bribe from a wealthy politician who had been interested in the murdered man's young wife. "But you did leave the Pinkertons, didn't you, Hatfield?"

"I quit them." Hatfield obviously didn't want to reminisce about Texas.

"Knew a Ranger who was in and around the case," Buchanan explained. "He had his notions."

Big Jim Cucamongo had not lost an iota of his beaming smile. "Well, let bygones be bygones, I always say. Shall we go inside, Buchanan? Coco will be anxious to see you."

The three officers of Los Angeles County promptly wheeled into position. They knew their business; nobody could possibly get at Big Jim Cucamongo from any angle. Buchanan fell in with them and went into the auditorium.

The theater was roomy, but it had the feeling Buchanan had noted in the hotel, that it was jerry-built, it lacked permanence. Rows of chairs were nailed together with furring lath. The audience, which consisted of no more than fifty people, was crowded down front close to the stage.

There was a prize ring set on the stage, but the ropes hung limp, and the proportions were all wrong. Foot-lamps burning coal-oil shed light on the stage. A buzz of voices came from the fans. Everyone looked up and applauded when Big Jim and his entourage came into view. The fat man bowed, beamed, and led the way up the steps and onto the stage, towing Buchanan along with him and the deputies.

The footlights interfered with Buchanan's vision. He shaded his eyes and looked backstage for Coco Bean, who was not in sight. A canvas curtain billowed slightly too near the ropes of the prize ring.

Big Jim Cucamongo was addressing the audience. "Ladeez and gentlemen . . . Just arrived in our fair city, one of the best known frontiersmen, sometime lawman, fighting hero . . . and manager of the challenger Coco Bean. . . . I give you Mr. Tom Buchanan!"

There was the sound of indifferent handclapping. A voice called, "Awright, Jim, let's see the battlers, now."

"Waited long enough," yelled another. "Bring on the meat."

"Now, friends." Cucamongo laughed heartily, as though all present were his good friends indeed. "You'll get to see your favorites spar, you'll get to pick your favorite for the betting. Don't you always get what Big Jim promises?"

"Yayyy! We do, we do!" It sounded suspiciously as if

it came from the men at the rear of the house, attired in the knitted jerseys that seemed to be a sort of uniform among supporters of the genial fat man, but others took it up, and there was appreciative laughter from the front rows.

Buchanan saw no good reason for being on stage. Pushing one of the deputies aside, he made for the wings as Cucamongo continued his easy-flowing address to the audience. Buchanan still squinted a bit from the glare of the reflectors behind the footlamps; therefore, he did not at once spot a huge figure of a man hurrying toward him.

This man was stripped to the waist. He wore long, tight-fitting drawers and soft shoes. A bright-colored blanket was slung over his shoulders. He had black hair, oriental eyes, and café au lait skin. Two men trotted behind him, carrying boxing gloves and other paraphernalia. From the stage, Big Jim was already announcing him: "Champion of the West, your own Chino Cruz!"

It seemed as though the great Chino Cruz was about to walk through Buchanan as though he were a shadow in the wing of the theater. The slanted eyes seemed not to see a human being in his path.

Buchanan lowered his shoulder. The prizefighter rammed into it. The contact was smashing. Buchanan felt great strength in the man, even as he applied pressure so that the blanket fell from the muscled torso. Chino Cruz thrust out a big fist.

Buchanan hit him with an inside right hand, going for the point where ribs and diaphragm met. The prizefighter stopped dead in his tracks.

Buchanan said, "One more time and you won't be able to go out there, big man. You want it . . . you get it."

Cruz was still catching his breath. He stood silent, staring, disbelieving.

Buchanan said, in the interest of psychology, "And Coco hits harder than that."

One of the handlers put the blanket back on the shoulders of Cruz. The oriental eyes brooded upon Buchanan.

"I fight for money." The voice was clear and cold.

"I'm Buchanan. I keep tryin' not to fight."

"I will kill your nigger."

Buchanan squinted at him. "Got a little of that blood in you, too, haven't you? Chinese, too? And Mexican?"

The pugilist seemed to swell to even larger proportions. "And you. I will take care of you later."

"Uh-huh," said Buchanan. "Now you run along and don't call names and be a good little boy or Big Jim will spank."

Chino Cruz's eyes flickered at last. The handlers were gently pushing at him. He strode past Buchanan and onto the stage. Cucamongo led the ovation. Cruz bowed with dignity. He was a man who believed in himself. There was a red mark on his body where Buchanan had hit him, but he did not know of it.

A tough man, Buchanan thought, walking down the corridor backstage, glancing back at the drop, noting there was space enough for a man behind the canvas that flanked the prize ring. A man not easy to knock about, able to take a good punch without going down; he would be a suitable opponent.

Coco Bean's voice called, "I know them footsteps. You got here at last, Tom Buchanan."

The dressing room was of ample proportions. Coco stood in the doorway, his eyes bright with pleasure. He was almost as tall as Buchanan, and his muscular development was that of a fighter; he had sloping shoulders, long arms, huge biceps, narrow hips, and good, shapely legs. He bore few scars of the profession. His white teeth were perfect.

"How you been, you rascal?"

Coco said, "Dumb, as usual. I can handle everything

but the contracts. This here is Judge Collyer. You talk to him."

Judge Collyer wore a spiked coat, a frilled white shirt, a stovepipe hat, and striped pants with straps that connected them to the arches of Congress boots. His collar and cuffs were clean. His eyes keenly examined Buchanan while his thin lips smiled. "Ah, yes. The manager. I was just this moment explaining to Mr. Bean his rights under the contract he signed with Mr. Cucamongo."

"The fine print," Coco said, shaking his head.

"You're Cucamongo's lawyer?" asked Buchanan.

"And a judge of the local courts. Ipso facto. Etcetera." Coco produced a somewhat shopworn document. "Should've waited until you got here, I reckon."

The legal form was elaborate, the script flowing, the seal officially witnessed and sealed with red wax. Buchanan glanced at it.

"A true agreement," said the judge. "Good in any court."

"You should know."

"Ah, yes. I drew it up. And it would come up before me, in my court." The judge fluffed at his Burnsides and smiled. "As I was explaining to Mr. Bean just now."

"Uh-huh."

"As Mr. Cucamongo requested. To prevent any further misunderstanding, you see."

"I see your point," said Buchanan. "However, maybe if you leave me alone, me and Coco?"

"Privacy is the prerogative of every citizen." Judge Collyer tapped his tall hat. "We shall meet again."

"Yea, verily," said Buchanan. He watched the dapper little man leave the room. He closed the door and leaned against it. "Now you better tell me about it."

Someone pushed against the door, and then hammered upon it, shouting, "Leave us in. Big Jim wants us in there."

"They my trainers," said Coco. "It's in the contract, to furnish me with trainers."

Buchanan suddenly stepped aside. The two men who had been shoving against the door catapulted into the room. They wore knit jerseys also, but of a bright red hue. They were quite unprepossessing. They spun around, and it could be seen that they were wearing revolvers in their belts.

"Trainers with guns," said Buchanan. "Odd, isn't it?"

"The way they do around here," said Coco. "They say it keeps the peace. That one's Sampson. The other's Dugan."

Buchanan eyed Dugan, a squat man with dull features. "You got a brother? A badge-wearer?"

"None of your business what I got," snarled Dugan.

"Yeah. None of your business," said Sampson.

Buchanan sighed. Then he made a quick move, collaring the two trainers. He brought their heads together smartly. He turned them against the nearest wall and extracted the guns from their belts.

Coco said, "They never done me anything. No way. They just stand around and keep people away from me. I ain't got to know a soul in this town."

Dugan growled, "We got orders. The fight's got to be on the level."

"Yeah," said Sampson. "Big Jim'll hear 'bout this."

Buchanan said, "Coco, open the door and holler for the boss, will you, please?"

Coco did as he was asked. The two men began to turn toward Buchanan. He swatted them back into position. He still had not read the contract. He picked it from the chair where he had tossed it while manhandling the trainers. He perused it down to the fine print, then handed it back to Coco.

"Sorta signed away your life," he said.

"That man sweet-talked me. He can do it real good. Promised me the world if I beat this man Chino."

"How many times have I warned you not to sign anything you can't read?"

"I can read it. I just didn't understand it," said Coco. "Not the way Judge Collyer tells it."

"Then you told them that I'm your manager. Which I ain't."

"I hadda do somethin'. So I sent for you. They ain't really done nothin', Tom. They gimme sparrin' partners— not much good, but good enough. They feed me. I sleep at a nice place. It's just—they make me nervous with their guns. You know how I hate guns."

"Everybody knows how you hate guns," said Buchanan. He heard Cucamongo approaching. He struck a wax match and held the contract over a cuspidor in a corner of the room. When the fat man came through the door the last of the document was turning to white ash. Buchanan said, "Didn't like the contract my fighter signed. So—you can forget about it."

Cucamongo looked at the ashes, then at the two guns Buchanan had removed and placed on the convenient chair, then at Coco, then back to Buchanan. And he laughed, freely, richly. "Come on, now, Buchanan. You can't hate a man for trying, can you?"

"Nope," said Buchanan. "Only you got no contract with me."

"But Coco didn't tell us about you until after he signed with me." Cucamongo shrugged, grinning. "I do have a copy, also signed by Coco. In my safe."

"But you wouldn't enforce it. I mean, Coco is entitled to training expenses and a share of the exhibition money. Winner take all, that's okay. But I take charge as of now."

"If you say so." Cucamongo's smile never faltered. "I'm not about to go against a popular character like you,

Buchanan. I know your reputation. I'm ambitious. I want you on my side."

"Uh-huh," said Buchanan. "Then we tear up that other contract, right? We begin all over again?"

"Whatever you say. Your name as a square shooter is my guarantee," said Cucamongo. "And Dugan and Sampson are fired."

"If you say so."

"All we want is a good fight. Exhibition, that is. Prize-fighting is illegal in these parts. But thanks to Judge Collyer we can put on exhibitions. And who is to prevent an un-biased referee from giving his opinion of the winner?"

"Oh, you don't have to worry about that," said Buchanan. "Coco knocks 'em out, all of 'em."

"That's just fine, if he can do it. There'll be plenty of betting action. It's a sporting proposition all the way."

"It may be. Now that the contract's burnt up. And one other little thing. I'll want an extra bed in my room. For Coco. I like to have him nearby when it's almost time for the bout."

Cucamongo finally blinked. "There's a hotel ruling . . ."

"But you do own the hotel."

"Of course. Sometimes I forget—I didn't always own property," said Cucamongo humbly, finding his smile again. "As you say, Buchanan. And we'll have a drink on it later, right?"

"After we count the take for the exhibition of sparrin' this afternoon," said Buchanan. "Right?"

"Right," said the fat man. He beamed at Coco. "I'll have your half ready when Chino finishes. Just you give us a good show now, you hear?"

"Yeah," said Coco. "I hear real good."

Cucamongo lifted a hand as if to bestow a benediction. "I'll be seeing you later."

He departed, still openly smiling and nodding. Coco stared at the closed door.

"Doggone, Tom, he's scared of you. He's eatin' right out of your hand."

"You think so?" Buchanan, shook his head soberly. "One thing I learned long ago. When a smart hombre starts givin' you the world with a fence around it . . . look out for trouble with a capital T."

"Aw, you plumb scared him, Tom."

"Don't ever believe it. That man's got Los Angeles somewhat tied up, treed. He's happy because he's strong. He's got that mealy-mouth judge plus an army of sneaky gents like your ex-trainers. Three of his men tried to kill Peter O'Brien yesterday. . . . Never mind that. Only those three wear badges. This is no piece of pie, Coco, my friend. This is tough all the way. You keep that in the front of your skull."

# Chapter 3

Pico House dominated the Plaza, the square upon which Los Angeles had been founded. The hotel was all of three stories high, but it was solidly built of native materials. Peter O'Brien walked back and forth in a room on the third floor. It was midafternoon, and he had accomplished nothing since his arrival that morning.

There was a tap on the door. He put his hand on the butt of a revolver in his waistband and asked, "Who is it?"

"Jenny."

He admitted her. She slid into the room and fell into a chair, circles beneath her eyes, proof of her exhaustion.

"No luck," he said. "It figured."

"Castellano's in Sacramento looking for help. Then he's going to San Francisco to talk to the money men."

"I heard about him. Doc Farrar's okay, but he's scared and helpless with Castellano away. They need all the Mexicans behind them. There are more white people

41

with Cucamongo than you could believe. He's got this town buffaloed."

"I know. He'll discover that we're in town. You know that. Any minute now we'll hear from him."

"I don't know about that. There's Buchanan."

"Oh, come on, now, Peter. Buchanan's not all that big."

On the chest of drawers, there was a bottle of the brandy made by the monks of Northern California. O'Brien opened his carpetbag and took out two small glasses and poured. He handed one to the woman and said, "He made you an offer. You better pay heed."

"You listened."

"I may not be as smart as Big Jim. But I ain't stupid."

"If you think Buchanan can get the best of it here in Los Angeles, you're not clever," she said wearily. "I'd help if I could."

"Buchanan's carryin' cash. He'll bet on Coco Bean."

"And lose."

"Maybe. But I'm goin' down with him. I'm goin' to bet the mortgage that Bean'll win."

"You're crazy, Peter."

"Could be." He sipped at the brandy "But if I win, I'll be in the clear when the cattle are sold and the crops are in. It's a last chance. And I know Buchanan."

"A big, ignorant cowboy with an overblown reputation," she said.

"Because he didn't fall for you like the rest of us?" Peter grinned at her. "Like even Mayor Castellano, who ain't around to help? Like all the men you blink at, includin' me?"

She said, "Sometimes you remind me of Tim."

"He wasn't jealous of you. Tim was a bad boy, but he wasn't jealous."

"No. But he had a nasty tongue."

"Okay," said O'Brien. "You listen to *this* nasty tongue: Buchanan is a man and a half and then some. He ain't only big, he's smart. I been to the ball with Buchanan. He ain't about to let his fighter take a beatin' from a big bum like Cruz. I'm goin' to bet on that. You want rail fare, you better nose around. Let Big Jim pat your—uh—hand if necessary. Or make up to one of his people. Bring the information to Buchanan, and you'll get what you want."

She showed no resentment at this. She tapped the brandy glass, sniffed at it. "You believe that, don't you?"

"You could say I gotta believe it. I seen Buchanan in action."

"A big, dumb cowhand," she mused. "Yes. It might be that he's the kind can handle Big Jim. One time, maybe."

"Okay. Then you get outa town, and what do you care?" He shrugged. "I know all you care about is gettin' back to New York, the theater. You told me often enough."

"And you'll have the ranch back, and you can hire guns to hold it." She nodded. "It's a nice picture."

"I can hold it and keep Big Jim away, long as I stay outa town and politics and such."

"Yes." she said. "You've got more fight and guts than Tim had. You could do it."

"So you go and do what you can. See Doc Farrar, he's soft on you, too. Talk to people."

She arose, swallowed the brandy. Color had returned to her cheeks. She said softly, "And prepare for a getaway just in case we lose? For all of us?"

"Might's well," he said. "There won't be anything left if we lose."

"We need sleep," she said. "I'll do as you say. Later."

"Lock your door good," he warned. "Big Jim'll be around."

"I know." She went without smiling, without a gesture. He laughed and propped a chair beneath the knob of the door, turned the key, and piled onto the bed.

She went out of the rear door of the hotel. They knew her in the Plaza. They knew the O'Briens, they hated

Cucamongo. They were older inhabitants, mainly of Mexican or Spanish descent—or both, with a mixture of Indian. Mayór Castellano was their man, they opted for law and order and a more equal share of the money coming into Los Angeles. They were no match for Big Jim.

She made her way through narrow, unpaved streets, driving deeper into the barrio, where the indigent Mexicans were forced to make their homes. There was a new frame building on a corner, near the westward limits of the section, indeed of the town. It stretched a hundred feet deep, narrow, one story high. She entered the front door in a rush, looking backward to make certain she was not followed.

Dr. Rudolph Farrar leaped up from behind a desk in a small, cluttered entry-room. He was a frail young man with sideburns that fluttered, a sensitive mouth, light blue eyes. His hands were those of a bigger man, strong, spatulate, always in motion.

"Jenny!"

"Yes, Rudolph. And, as usual, in need of help."

"Of course. Is there anyone—are you in danger?" He stepped toward a corner where there leaned, incongruously, a double-barreled shotgun; next to it was a canvas stretcher attached to long poles and a skeleton suspended from a wooden rack.

She let herself shrink, playing the frightened waif to his Galahad. "I—I think not. I tried to avoid them."

"Cucamongo," he said. "O'Brien."

"Not Peter," she breathed, leaning against a wall, shoulders drooping. "The other, yes. I must talk with you, Rudolph. And—I need sleep. We rushed to town without going to bed last night."

"Castellano won't return until next week," he said. "There is no one else."

"We know . . . Peter is trying to fight back, now. This

man Buchanan. . . . We must talk."

"Sleep," he said. "You shall have my bed. He tapped a bell upon his desk and a handsome young Negro woman came from the hospital proper, nodded at Jenny, sharp-eyed, suspicious, solicitous of the doctor. "Please change my linen and see that Mrs. O'Brien has a gown. She needs sleep very badly, as you can see."

The nurse's name was Nellie Franklin. She nodded without enthusiasm and departed. She worked long hours for little pay, learning medicine from Dr. Farrar; she was a dedicated young woman whose doubts about Jenny O'Brien were obvious at all times when they met at the hospital.

Jenny said, "You're always so kind, Rudolph."

He flushed. "You are aware of my sentiments, Jenny."

"I'm sorry." She covered her face with her hands. "I must try to rebuild my life. I must return to my home. New beginnings, only a new start will help."

"Yes. I have heard you say it so often, I know it is true."

"You are so kind, so understanding." She tottered toward him, resting her head upon his shoulder.

The good, strong hands became all thumbs. He did not know what to do with them. He held her loosely, murmuring to her. "You should go away from this raw environment, you are quite right. You belong in civilization, among people of good manners and intentions. . . ."

From the doorway, Nurse Nellie Franklin said dryly, "The bed's all ready, doctor."

He led the clinging, fragile Jenny to his private quarters. Nurse Nellie made a face, pursed her lips, and uttered a slight, buzzing sound, denoting disbelief and dislike, plus a great deal of distaste.

Cucamongo had built his office adjacent to the bar of the hotel; it was a spacious room that had a second door leading to the alley, on the opposite side of which was the door to the Coliseum. This was a handy arrangement after dark and some of the time in the afternoon when he wished to move quickly and quietly about his business. It was a huge room, with a rolltop desk, a comfortable couch, several chairs and throw-rugs on the floor, and Western scenes in frames on the wall. He sat behind the desk, dominating the others who gathered to drink his whiskey and listen to his words of wisdom.

Judge Carroll was there, and Hatfield the bird dog, and Chino Cruz in a corner, silent and sweating after the workouts. Dugan and Wilks nursed beers and were for the most part silent and rather glum.

The judge said, "This man Buchanan. Arrogant, I'd say."

"A figure up and down the frontier," said Cucamongo. "Hatfield knows all about him."

"Damn dangerous," said the former Pinkerton. "I sort of worked with him once, then against him. Today . . ." He broke off, coughed, glanced at the judge, "well, he surprised me, in a way."

"A figure of romance. His name means much to the common people," said the judge. "But an arrogant man."

"His name," agreed Cucamongo. "A good name. What if it were to be brought down? Smirched?"

"A good thing for the benighted West," said Carroll.

"Right," agreed Hatfield. "You want things to be run right, you got to get rid of people like Buchanan."

"Barbarians. Indian lovers," said Judge Carroll. "Guns are all they know. Uncivilized."

"Precisely," said Cucamongo. "I come from the East, where law and order is everything. That's what I stand for, a decent city kept clean by the good people."

Hatfield batted his eyes but declined to comment. Dugan and Wilks shifted uneasily but also kept silence. Chino Cruz seemed half-asleep.

"Buchanan's kind was good enough when this was a desert and San Pedro a fishing village," said the judge. "Now we are on the threshold of great growth. Los Angeles will be the city of Southern California, rivaling San Francisco. Ruffians with no respect for legal documents have no place in our future."

"Nor niggers, nor greasers." Cucamongo was riding his hobby horse. "Eyetalians is different, you can trust 'em. My father was Eyetalian, a fine man back in New York."

Chino Cruz opened one eye. Hatfield and the deputies were looking his way. He closed the eye again. He had learned his lesson long since, keep the mouth shut, obey orders, and survive.

Judge Carroll said sententiously, "Julius Caesar was an Italian."

"Yeah," smirked Cucamongo. "I knew that. Michael Angelo, too." He looked condescendingly at Hatfield. "These here were great men in their day."

Hatfield said, "I heard about 'em. Just make me chief of police when you get to be mayor. I'll take care of things."

"You will. You will." Big Jim chuckled. Hatfield would do anything in the world to be restored to power over those who broke laws, any laws. Hatfield was the best man-hunter in America if given his own way to go—a useful tool. "So now we get some more money in the war chest with this fight. We take care of Buchanan one way or another."

Hatfield said quickly, "Leave him to me."

"If you're smart, like I said. No use to make him look good. Destroy his reputation and maybe you won't even have to kill him. Maybe we can put him on the run."

"I'll think about it," Hatfield promised. "It can be done."

Judge Carroll arose, adjusted the stovepipe pants,

shined a boot on each skinny calf. "Yes. Well, justice will triumph, never you fear. My life on it, gentleman. And good evenin' to you all."

He strutted out, a small man of no particular ability, a jackleg lawyer who had made the correct moves in his middle years and now sat on the bench. Hatfield grunted, looking after him.

"There's one could go along with Castellano," he said.

"He's a nobody . . . but he's our nobody," Big Jim said. "Everything in its time and place, Hatfield."

"Yeah, you're right." But Hatfield was dissatisfied.

There was a tap on the door leading to the barroom. Dugan and Wilks faced around, hands on their guns. Hatfield opened the door a crack. Durand, the bartender, spoke.

"Buchanan and O'Brien and the nigger."

"Send 'em in," said Cucamongo. "Make 'em welcome." His eyes went around the room. Chino straightened up, the two deputies took positions which would cover their boss in case of any contingency. "Don't make a bad move, now. They'll be peaceable. Stay cool."

O'Brien came in first, restored by sleep and food, a bit cocky, glancing quickly around, nodding to all in turn. Coco followed, unsmiling, taking up space nearest Hatfield, where he could watch the other deputies. Buchanan closed the door behind him, shutting out Durand.

"Gentleman," he said. "Top of the evening."

They muttered responses as Cucamongo arose and extended a hand. O'Brien refused it but Buchanan accepted the meaningless gesture for what it was.

Cucamongo said, "How about a drink, gents?"

"Rather get to business first," Buchanan said. "Peter, here, he wants to make a bet, so he tells me. Wants witnesses."

Cucamongo said, "Well, there's enough of us here. What you got to bet, Peter?"

"Enough," said O'Brien. "What I got left of the ranchero. The works."

Cucamongo said carefully, "You mean you want to bet your stake in the ranch against the mortgage? Is that it?"

"That's it. I got a little odds comin', I think."

Cucamongo shook his head. "You got no cash, Peter. I consider it an even bet."

"If you win, you own the place."

"I expect to own it by foreclosure," said Cucamongo without emphasis, almost gently. "You've been unwise, Peter."

"Yeah, but I'm offerin' you the bet." O'Brien pointed to Coco. "I'm bettin' on him, everybody got that straight?"

Hatfield said, "We hear you."

"Agreed. At evens," said Cucamongo.

O'Brien looked to Buchanan, who shrugged a huge shoulder. Then he said, "Okay. Evens. It's a bet."

Cucamongo asked, "Mr. Buchanan? Your pleasure."

Buchanan said, "I've got a thousand in cash. Trouble is, who holds the stakes?"

"Why, the purse is in my safe. Plenty of people are placing their stakes at the bar."

"With Durand?" Buchanan shook his head. "I know that jasper. You want to take my word for a thousand, I'll sign an agreement. But I part with no cash for Durand to hold."

"If I assume the responsibility?" Cucamongo scowled for the first time. It altered his appearance considerably, he suddenly looked hard and angered.

Buchanan said, "Look at it any old way you want. There's witnesses, like you said. I'll show you that I got the cash."

He dropped a leather sack on Cucamongo's desk. The contents clinked with the authority of gold coins, a sound different from other sounds.

The fat man hesitated, then resumed his customary oily, smiling manner, "I believe you, Buchanan. Your word is good enough for me. I am sorry mine is not good enough for you."

"Oh, I'm not questioning your word," said Buchanan. "It's Durand, remember? You hire a known crook and you got to expect people to be a bit wary. Right?"

"Durand came highly recommended," said Cucamongo. "He's been efficient and honest as a bartender."

"And as a dealer?"

"We don't know him as a dealer."

"You might ask Hatfield," said Buchanan. "He knows Durand. Maybe he recommended him."

He had scored, it was plain. The two men lost their aplomb for a moment, recovered as Buchanan grinned at them.

Hatfield said. "Don't worry, Buchanan. You got your bet. Everybody in this burg knows Big Jim's good for it."

"Uh-huh," said Buchanan.

Peter O'Brien was not satisfied. "That's what they told my brother Tim."

The atmosphere changed in an instant. The deputies braced themselves, Hatfield's eyes went cold, Cucamongo straightened at his desk. O'Brien's remark could have meant the beginning of real trouble.

"Your brother Tim asked for what he got," Hatfield said flatly. "I looked into that. He was drunk and disorderly."

Cucamongo added, "He was a loser, Peter. You know that."

"I heard he was winnin' the night he was murdered," O'Brien said.

"He was not," said Hatfield. "I looked into that."

"You? I wouldn't trust you across this room," said O'Brien. "Jim's got some kind of a conscience, I do believe. But you? Never."

Buchanan said, "If our business is completed I'd admire to leave, Peter."

Coco murmured, "Yeah. There's too many guns in this here room."

O'Brien said, "I've said all this before. Just wanted to make it clear where I stand."

"See you after the fight," said Cucamongo. He held onto his smile, winking at Buchanan, friendly. "It'll be a big night for Los Angeles."

"Uh-huh," said Buchanan. "Big night for the gamblin' people. Come on, Peter."

He gently pushed O'Brien out the door. Coco followed closely behind the angry rancher. Buchanan paused, looked around.

"Nice place you got here, Cucamongo. Hatfield, keep it in line, you hear? Wouldn't want any real hooraw now, would we?"

Hatfield said, "No trouble."

Buchanan lifted a hand, grinned and closed the door behind him. Everyone relaxed, changing position as though they felt cramped. Hatfield swore under his breath.

"I'll get him some day."

"Maybe," said Cucamongo. "First, we got to make sure we win this fight. That's first, remember what I say."

"Ain't no problem if your man does his job," said Hatfield.

Chino said automatically, "I'll murder him."

"You do as you're told," Cucamongo snapped. All the sugary friendliness had evaporated now. "You do exactly what you're supposed to do, understand?"

The huge prizefighter drew a deep breath. Then he said in a subdued voice, "Yeah. I understand."

"I don't want any mistakes made, now or later. Bad enough what happened yesterday on El Camino Real."

"Buchanan," growled Hatfield. "How'd we know he'd be on deck?"

"You missed him," Cucamongo said. "We may have a lot of trouble because you missed him."

Hatfield did not flinch. "Dugan and Silk were in my line of fire. Buchanan was hittin' for the brush. When I miss it's because of a reason, understand that."

Cucamongo scowled but refrained from comment. He made a gesture, and they all moved for the door. He wanted to be alone, to put his mind to work. His strength lay in working out every possible angle of every upcoming situation.

He knew what he wanted. He wanted to build Los Angeles into a mighty city—astride which he would stand, riches and power in his grasp. He wanted the woman, Jenny O'Brien. And then he could look northward toward the seat of government, the nabobs of San Francisco, for further conquest.

Some day, he thought, some day he would make it. Big Jim was born to rule . . . like Julius Caesar.


Buchanan and O'Brien walked the streets in the dark of night. O'Brien complained that he was thirsty, that he had brandy in his room where they could talk and later get something to eat.

Buchanan said, "I'm hungrier than you are, you can figure that any time. But walls sometimes have ears."

"Jim don't cut any ice at Pico House."

"But he might hire someone that does," said Buchanan. "You got to know this man is smart. What we got to wonder is how he is making sure his man beats Coco."

"With both of us in the corner we can watch out for doped water and all," said O'Brien. "I can't see any other way. They got a referee will favor 'em, but you say Coco will knock him out."

"Coco knocks out anyone he fights," Buchanan said.

"Thing is, they're figurin' on kayoin' Coco. But how?"

"I dunno how. I'm thirsty." The truth was that unless he had a touch of booze every hour or so he became shaky. He had been hitting the bottle a lot since Tim's death and the bad luck that had closed in upon him.

Buchanan said, "I got a notion."

"You want to tell me about it?"

"No. I might be wrong. Just you watch the corner with me during the bout. I'll tell you when to make a move."

"The whole town'll be against us."

"I know." Buchanan looked down at the smaller man. "You had the nerve to bet your ranch. You'll need a lot more before this is over."

"I'll be there with you."

And a bottle in your pocket, Buchanan thought, but he said aloud, "Now, what about Jenny?"

"What do you mean?"

"Well, where is she?"

"Huntin' around for any information that might help."

"You sure she's on our side?"

"She's got to be. Otherwise Cucamongo'll grab her off and make her like it."

"Does she know that?"

"She really knows it. She don't scare easy, but she's scared of Big Jim. She was gettin' onto Tim there, before the end, but she purely hates Jim."

"She did turn against your brother, though?"

"Not as far as outsiders was concerned. But I knew. Tim wasn't much good for a woman."

"Handsome and full of fun, wasn't he?"

"Oh, sure. He could get the women. But over the long haul—he didn't do so good. She wanted to go back east before he was killed."

"I see." It explained some about the woman. She felt free despite the fact that her husband had been murdered. She would avenge him if she had the opportunity to do it without danger to herself, mainly because of her hatred of Cucamongo. It wasn't much to lean on.

"Let's go to Pico House," said O'Brien. "There's nothin' else important to talk about."

He was correct, Buchanan thought as they changed direction and started back toward the Plaza. And talking to Peter O'Brien could well be whistling up the chimney. There was an aura of desperation about the man. He was not cowardly, but he was harassed. To depend upon him in a tight spot would be dangerous, Buchanan thought.

And yet there was nobody else. The woman was even more a risk, he believed. He was slowly beginning to get a picture of her. She was all for Jenny O'Brien, no doubt about it, but then so were most people out for number one. What bothered Buchanan was that she adopted too many faces, that where she really stood at any given moment could not be fathomed.

He thought of the many ways a fight could be fixed. He eliminated the most obvious—drugs—because they had made no effort to tamper with Coco's training. They would have caused a gradual breakdown to make him vulnerable to such raw attempts. No, it was something special, something they thought original and safe from detection.

He again thought of the canvas curtain on the stage of the theater, as he had many times since he had spotted it. The key lay in its juxtaposition to the ropes, he thought. It must be that, and it was not original. He had seen he same trick pulled in a circus tent, years before in South Dakota.

So he would continue to ponder, and he would wear his gun in the corner the night of the bout. It was against his principles, but he would do it, because he foresaw trouble.

But tonight he would eat at the hotel whether O'Brien drank whiskey or not. He was hungry—and a bit worried in this strange town among so many dubious characters.

# Chapter 4

It was the afternoon of the great prizefight in Los Angeles. Coco was sleeping, peaceful as a baby. There was a light tap on the door of Room 222 of the Coliseum Hotel. Buchanan answered, his revolver ready on his hip, his eye alert.

Tomás the bellboy slipped into the room. "The señora sends for you."

"Señora O'Brien?"

"She is at the hospital. If she is not, you are to look for her, since she will be in danger."

"You mean she will be at the hospital." He had heard of Dr. Farrar and his good deeds and had located the building just in case medical aid was needed before they got out of town. He had not laid eyes on Jenny since the night at the hacienda.

"Just what I have said." Tomás was solemn. "My people, they have bet all they own on Mr. Coco."

Buchanan nodded. "I heard. Can you keep an eye on this room while I look for the señora?"

"There are others who will help," said the youth. "You do not know them. Best you should not."

"Uh-huh," said Buchanan. "A man can own part of a city, but he can't own all of it."

"He cannot own all the people," said Tomás in Spanish. "That is what keeps us alive through hope."

"As you say." Buchanan went out with the boy, locking the door behind him.

As he walked the streets, people greeted him, some surreptitiously, some openly, some mockingly. He had become known over night as the manager of Coco Bean, the well-advertised frontiersman, Indian fighter, scout, and lawman. He did not enjoy it, but the newspaper had made a sensational story of his alleged past.

At the hospital, he found Dr. Farrar in his waiting room. He asked for the woman.

"You are Buchanan." The slender young man extended a strong, graceful hand.

"Yeah. She was supposed to have some information for me. If so, I owe her money."

The doctor bit his lip. "She has been seeking. But I fear she is now with Cucamongo. If so—she is in danger."

Buchanan asked, "At the Coliseum? I just came from there."

"No. I believe it is at Pico House. She . . . she was a bit desperate."

Buchanan said, "Then she has no information."

"If so she has not confided in me." Farrar was controlled but tense.

Buchanan said, "I'll mosey over there."

"If there's anything I can do . . ."

"Be ready to receive bodies," Buchanan said grimly. "In any case, there'll be bodies to care for."

He walked swiftly to the Plaza. He went up the stairs three at a time to O'Brien's room. Peter was asleep, exhaling the fumes of California brandy. The door was slightly open.

Buchanan nudged the sleeping figure. "You're sure a trustin' soul."

O'Brien dug a knuckle into his eyes. "Uh—Jenny. You seen Jenny?"

"Just about to ask you that question."

"She showed up today. Says she's been stayin' at Doc Farrar's hospital. Been nosin' around at night with some kid from the hotel. Tomás?"

"Tomás," said Buchanan. "Good boy, I think. In this town, it's mighty hard to tell."

"So we had a couple drinks. More'n she usually takes." He shook his head hard. "I'd already had some. . . . Then she said she was goin' to tackle Cucamongo and I shouldn't do nothin' about it."

"But she sent for me."

O'Brien rolled off the bed. He steadied himself with one hand on the bureau, found the brandy bottle, obviously not the first, since this one was nearly full, and took a sip. "We better check her room."

"You'd best stay right here," said Buchanan. "I want you stone sober at the fight, you hear me? Cold, flat sober."

"Yeah. You're right." He poured water in the basin on the commode and dipped his face into it. "Yeah. She was in the room down two doors. That way." He pointed. "What can I tell you about that beauty?"

"Not a thing," said Buchanan.

"Cucamongo won't be alone. Supposin' I cover the hall?"

"Just don't leave this room," said Buchanan. "I need you at the fight. I think I know now exactly what they mean to try."

O'Brien winked; for a moment he was the old, hell-bent for-leather man Buchanan had known in the past.

"We was at that circus together. The tent with the rassler?"

"You mind that."

"Surest thing y' know. The big-town kid was doin' right good when the circus rassler got his head against the canvas wall."

"And someone swung a hammer on his skull."

"Right." O'Brien sobered. "You got to be in Coco's corner to watch out for drugs. You want me backstage?"

"Is there anyone else we could trust?"

"Nope." He thought a moment. "Mebbe Jenny, but that's no good."

"She's got to know about it, though."

"Yeah. She's got to know."

Buchanan said, "So lay off the booze. I'll talk to her."

"You do that," said O'Brien. "I'll oil up my gun."

"I wish we didn't have to tote 'em. Guns in town are always bad," said Buchanan. "But this is a time for it."

"You can bet your boots on it," said O'Brien. "You want to tell Jenny about it?"

"I'll tell her right now."

"If you can find her."

"If I can't . . . I'll be back here. Otherwise, see you tonight." He looked hard at O'Brien. "No brandy, mind you."

"Like you say." O'Brien grinned. "There'll be trouble enough later."

Buchanan edged the door open and peered into the hall. He saw shadowy movement to his left. Taking a deep breath, he motioned for O'Brien to yank open the door. He poised, then burst through it, O'Brien close behind him; he saw a blur of movement and spun around.

Dugan and Wilks were converging on him. Buchanan caught them, one in each hand. He brought their heads together with a dull *thunk*. They wilted; he set them against the wall and turned to look for Hatfield. O'Brien was scanning the hall, gun in hand.

"Two doors this way?" asked Buchanan.

"Right down there," said O'Brien.

Buchanan made no secret of his movement, pounded upon the heavy panel of the door to Jenny's room. "Buchanan here. Open up."

There was no reply for the moment, but he had the feeling that the room was occupied. O'Brien was watching the deputies beginning to slide down the wall like two sacks of grain, coming to a seated position, legs stretched out in front of them.

Buchanan tried the knob of the door. It was locked. He called, "I'm goin' to shoot off the latch in another minute."

There was a rustling within the room. Buchanan stepped back, alert. O'Brien divided his attention between the semiconscious deputies and the door to Jenny's room.

Cucamongo came into the hallway. His face was pink, his jaw set. He stared at Buchanan, then at O'Brien and the two men sprawled on the floor.

"What's all this?" he demanded. "I don't take this kindly, gentlemen. I truly don't."

O'Brien said, "The hell you do," but Buchanan had an immediate sense of defeat. Cucamongo was too confident, too smooth in his speech and manner.

The door swung wider. Jenny stood within the room. She was dressed in a flowing robe—a costume more suitable for the boudoir than the street.

She said, "Really, Peter . . . Mr. Buchanan . . . This is an intrusion, isn't it?"

"Uh-huh," said Buchanan while O'Brien stared numbly. "Sure is. My mistake altogether. Y'all excuse me."

He took O'Brien's elbow and steered him back down the hall and into his room. He closed the door and mopped his brow with a kerchief.

"Whew! Reckon I'll take a snort of that brandy, now."

"What the hell?" demanded O'Brien.

Buchanan poured the liquor, drank it straight down. "You know her better'n I do. Way I heard it, she hated him, was scared of him."

"She was." O'Brien scratched his jaw. "I swear to you, she was. I don't know what game she thinks she's playin' now. One thing, it's dynamite. He may be foolish about her, but that's where it ends."

"Correct." Buchanan put down the glass. He went into the hall again. The deputies were struggling to their feet. They stared at him, still a bit cross-eyed. He wagged a finger at them. "Naughty, naughty. Just stand there, now. Don't move around, you'll make me nervous."

The door to Jenny's room was closed again. O'Brien joined Buchanan and locked the room. There was no reason to linger longer, Buchanan thought.

He said, "You boys be real careful now. Take good care of your boss. See you later."

The deputies mumbled. O'Brien walked beside Buchanan down the stairs and out onto the Plaza. People strolled about, none in much of a hurry. Many were Mexicans. A woman sold tacos from a barrow, and children played in the dusty streets. It was a pleasant scene on a warm day in late November.

O'Brien said, "Women are the devil."

"All folks is critters, my daddy always said." Buchanan paused to buy apples from a laden fruit stand. "Could be Jenny's got plans."

"Money," said O'Brien. "She wants that train fare back to New York. She wants it real bad. Worse'n I even thought, it seems."

"I've known women to do worse for money," said Buchanan. "It's more'n that. She's got it in her mind and her heart, that trip back to her home."

"Home?" O'Brien thought a moment. "Yeah. It is her home. Makes a bit of difference, don't it?"

"Some." Buchanan led the way around to the back of

the hotel and stopped at the stable where Nightshade was being cared for. The Mexican boy appeared, grinning. "You exercise him some, boy?"

"Si, senor. Tomás, he tell me."

"Uh-huh," said Buchanan. "Glad to have you on our side."

The youth shrugged, spreading open hands. Buchanan went into the stable. Nightshade whinnied, half-welcoming, half-protesting at being cooped up so long. Buchanan went into the stall and produced the apples. The big black snuffled his approval, chomping away.

"Gentle like a kitten," the boy said. "So big, so gentle."

"Just don't try to ride him," Buchanan told him.

"Your man, he win?" The boy gestured with fists. "We bet. Ten dollas, all I got."

Buchanan said in Spanish, "You bet on the proper man."

"Ah, sí. Tomás say, ev-body bet."

"Good."

They left the stable. They walked to the hotel and went into the bar, which was jammed. Money flashed as men placed their bets with Durand. Hatfield sat on a high stool, smiling gently, the peace officer doing his duty, maintaining order among the citizenry as they played at games.

Buchanan said, "I wouldn't put up a dime with that thief Durand. We better go up and see how it is with Coco."

Tomás spoke from his favorite spot behind the potted tree. "Señor . . . it is all clear. I have been watching."

Buchanan dug in a pocket and found a gold piece. "Been meanin' to see you got this. Don't bet it all on the fight tonight, now, will you?"

"I already bet all," said Tomás. "My people, they are betting as on a cockfight. Which is all the way."

"Coco is good enough to win, that's true."

Tomás made a face. "I did not say all my people bet on Coco Bean. Some believe Big Jim, he cannot ever lose."

"Uh-huh. That figures," said Buchanan. He led O'Brien up the stairs and knocked on the door of 222 before using his key, making sure Coco knew who was entering.

He may as well have saved his knuckles. The brown, relaxed body sprawled on the bed, the afternoon sunlight playing on the long, smooth muscles.

"You see how worried he is," remarked Buchanan. "That's my friend, always frettin'."

"You sure he knows just what to do?"

"He knows."

Coco opened an eye, grinned. "Spin him to the canvas."

"You see?" Buchanan looked at his watch. "Time to eat your fruit."

Coco said, "Rather have a juicy steak and trimmin's."

"That's what I eat today," said Buchanan. "For you, fruit until after the fight."

Coco took an apple from a platter and gnawed at it. He winked at Peter O'Brien. "Tom, he's a real boss man. A slave driver. Me, I know about slaves."

"Uh, yeah," said O'Brien, uncomfortable. "Uh—you know we got a lot bet on you tonight. You got to make the right move at the right time."

Coco asked, "Is it all right if I knock him out before I have to make a move like that?"

"Any old time you knock him out is okay with me," said O'Brien. "When I saw you first I knew you were good. When Tom came and told me about you I was satisfied."

"Uh-huh," said Buchanan. "So you say. Now tell me, why did you and Jenny come in here without sleepin' last night?"

O'Brien did not meet his eyes. "Well, the booze. And she had notions. I mean, she figured Big Jim would have it fixed, and she wanted to know everything. . . .You know how she is."

"I'm learnin'," said Buchanan. "And you didn't want me around to butt in. Right?"

"Well, she wanted to get here first. I don't know . . . ask her."

Buchanan said, "She's really got a hold on you and Big Jim and all, hasn't she now?"

"You'll learn. Maybe," said O'Brien.

"Not if I can help it," Buchanan told him.

There was a tap on the door. Buchanan motioned to O'Brien to stand aside; Coco moved toward a corner. "Who's there?"

"Me. Jenny."

Still cautious, he opened the door a crack, revolver in hand. She swept past him, clad in a long, dark cloak, a bonnet concealing her face. Coco snatched at a blanket to cover his nude body.

Buchanan said, "Got through with the big man, huh? He send you here?"

"Yes," she said, staring at him. She produced from beneath the cloak a vial of cloudy liquid. "I'm to see that this goes into Coco's water bottle."

Buchanan took it from her. "He pay you well?"

"He didn't pay me . . . yet."

"I see. So . . . how you expect to earn the money?"

"I don't. I expect to get it from you."

"Uh-huh," said Buchanan. "Thought it would come down to that."

"I'm giving it to you. There's a night train."

Buchanan reached into his pocket. He took out a bag of gold coins he liked to keep loose for emergencies. He placed eagles into her palm, one by one, watching her face. She was flushed and eager. She made a cup of both hands as he finished paying her, then went to the table, piled the coins in a heap, took out a silken purse with a drawstring, and filled it with the gold. Her eyes shone; she smiled like a bride at the altar.

Buchanan asked, "Are you going to wait for the fight?"

"Why should I?" she demanded.

"If Chino wins you might collect from Big Jim."

She bit her lip. "I hadn't thought of that."

"Uh-huh," said Buchanan. "You'll never make a good crook if you don't cover all the angles."

She whirled, glaring. "I'm not a crook."

"Big Jim might think different."

"He had my husband killed! I have a right to . . . do what I must to get home to New York."

"Okay," said Buchanan. "So you gave us the bottle, here. We paid for it. The rest is up to you."

She pondered, not looking at them, walking to the window. "Yes. I could collect. From him."

"You have to take the chance he'll . . . harm you."

"Harm me?" She smiled at them now. "Why, this afternoon he asked me to marry him."

O'Brien hooted. "Marry him? Oh, no!"

"Oh, yes. He has a great future. Mayor, maybe even governor of the state. He said so. He's got everything. Money, influence, a future. As Mrs. Cucamongo I would be the first lady of the land."

O'Brien said, "And you turned him down?"

Her eyes flashed fire. "Damn you, Peter O'Brien! I married your worthless brother for love. You know that. And you, Mr. Tom Buchanan, with your suspicions and your muscles. And all of you. I'd rather be a scrubwoman in New York than queen of all your miserable Western country!"

She swept to the door, yanked it open and departed, leaving the three men speechless and somewhat breathless. Coco swallowed the last of a pear and remarked, "That's one time I was left out and didn't mind a single bit."

"Whew," said O'Brien. "I seen her mad before . . . but not that mad."

"She did say 'all of you,' " Buchanan reminded him. He uncorked the bottle she had given him. He smelled its contents, then took a sip. He made a wry face. "Laudanum. In the water bottle it would slow a man down for the kayo. Big Jim wasn't takin' any chances."

"He covered it good," said O'Brien. "You reckon he's got somethin' else up his sleeve?"

"If he hasn't, he can make one up as we go along. Like I say, never underestimate a Cucamongo," Buchanan said. "We better stay right here, have Tomás bring up our food, be careful of what we eat."

"Let Tomás tell 'em it's for somebody else," suggested O'Brien. "If we're doped it'll be as bad as if Coco drank the laudanum."

"Good notion," said Buchanan. "Better run down and tell Tomás. It's gettin' later every minute."

When O'Brien had departed on his errand, Coco looked at Buchanan with raised eyebrows. "You believe he's on the level?"

"Not any more than he has to be," said Buchanan. "Right now it's to his advantage to level with us."

"I got us into a den of thieves," mourned Coco. "Way I heard it, this was a fine place, just gettin' rich, plenty of money around, all that."

"There's plenty of money," said Buchanan. "Trouble is, Big Jim Cucamongo's corraled most of it."

"Supposin' we take some, you think we'll get out of town alive?"

"Only if we're smart and quick."

"Guns," said Coco dismally. "I see it comin'. More shootin'. It never fails to wind up with guns."

"In this city, at this time, we'd be in a tough fix without 'em," Buchanan told him. "You've had enough of that fruit. Jog up and down a little. Can't have you goin' in there with anything roilin' in your stomach."

Coco dutifully trotted in place. He was always amenable in training, never fidgety or temperamental. In fact, he was never really out of condition, since he did not smoke or drink. He was a gentle soul, a good man in every way, Buchanan ruminated. It was not his fault they had fallen into a dangerous situation. No one could possibly know about Big Jim Cucamongo without coming into actual conflict with him.

California bred fruit and vegetables large in size. Its villains prospered equally in the salubrious climate, Buchanan decided.

# Chapter 5

The Coliseum Theater was jammed. The crowd was unlike any Buchanan had ever seen, flashy women mixed in with men of means and sporting characters, and wildly cheering Mexicans filled the rear rows. The demand for seats had been great, and all the orchestra rows had been reserved for "friends of Big Jim." Politics was rife even at this semilegal sporting event.

Three black-clad nuns moved down the aisles with alms-boxes, reaping a small harvest from the pleasure-bent assemblage. Two were small, one was tall. Buchanan, scanning every individual as the semifinal bout between middleweights was coming to an end, suddenly stiffened.

"Hey, Peter. Look there. At that tall nun."

O'Brien squinted from the wings. "Holy cow! It's her!"

"She claims to be an actress," said Buchanan. "I believe her. She actually looks . . . uh . . . humble out there!"

Jenny O'Brien was accepting a coin, bowing her head, making a feeble religious gesture to her patrons in the aisle seats. The man passed the box along and others dropped money through the slot.

"The church'll never see those contributions," O'Brien predicted. "That'll be eatin' money when she gets to New York."

Coco was jigging beneath a heavy woolen sweater, his legs clad in long tights, around his waist an American flag. He said, "It's a sin to steal from church."

"That woman ain't above sin," growled O'Brien.

In the ring, the brown-skinned Mexican boy launched a quick, two-handed attack against a sallow, freckled, bowlegged opponent and knocked him down. From the back seats, people howled with glee. Cigar smoke rose in a cloud, concealing the aisles for a moment as the wealthy puffed to cover their rage and disappointment at losing a few bets. The referee was a burly man named Joe Royce. He counted very slowly, but the prone man showed no disposition to get up.

Buchanan asked, "You got the sweat up, Coco?"

"I got it. Still don't think that lady oughta steal from the church," said Coco.

"Don't fret about that. Think of this big Chino Cruz and what you got to remember," urged Buchanan. "And don't charge out there like a bull. I told you that a hundred times. Tonight it could get you killed."

"I like to go to them," said Coco simply. "I like to show 'em who's the boss."

"Not this time," Buchanan begged, knowing that when the bell sounded Coco could go wild and start punching. He turned to O'Brien, saw that he was sweating. "Check back of that curtain. And keep your wits about you, Peter, if you ever did."

O'Brien leaned against the back wall of the stage. They were taking the defeated boxer out this side, the eyes of the handlers sliding sideways, then straight ahead as they went by, the tip-off to anyone with a grain of sense that something was going on, Buchanan thought. He watched Big Jim come out in all the glory of a cutaway coat and begin the announcement of the big event.

The tall nun came from the stage at the right rear. She brushed close to Buchanan and whispered, "I must pretend that I am close enough to put the potion in Coco's bottle."

"Uh-huh," said Buchanan, not entirely trusting her, wondering at her chameleon-like changes of attitude. When they had last seen her, she had berated them; now her voice was low, calm, cool.

Big Jim concluded, "And now, folks, the two best heavyweight boxers in the world . . . in an exhibition of the fistic art. . . . Here they are! Coco Bean, the black champion . . ."

O'Brien skipped back to take care of the pail and the water bottle. He glared at Jenny, said to Buchanan, "All clear for now. Nobody back there. Deputies standin' guard to make sure only the right people get to be there."

Buchanan said, "Just be ready."

Jenny O'Brien was close to them for a long moment. Then she went down into the audience and across the front row to the other side of the theater. She walked past Cucamongo, and Buchanan, ever watchful of all, saw the big man start, stare, then grin as she kept going out of sight.

So now the plot was to look for Coco to sag under the influence of drugs—or to be shoved against the loose ropes of the ring, his head making a dent in the canvas backdrop, so that he could then be knocked semiconscious by a blow delivered from the space between the curtain and the back wall of the stage. It was all very clear and simple, Buchanan thought. Cucamongo had covered every angle by having his deputies on hand. Hatfield, the most trustworthy of the henchmen, would handle the mallet in back of the curtain.

Buchanan spoke again to Coco as they went into the glare of the kerosene lamps. "Remember, please. Remember what we agreed. Play it for all it's worth."

Coco said, "Lady shouldn't steal from the church. She collects that money wearin' them clothes, she should turn it over to a preacher."

"Priest," said Buchanan, sighing. Coco sometimes got caught in a thought like this and lost his concentration. "She may be lookin' for a priest right now."

"Best she does. She won't git to heaven if she don't," said Coco darkly.

"Will you pay attention?" Buchanan was wearing his gunbelt, the holster tied down on his flank. O'Brien was carrying a small revolver in his pocket. Still, they were vulnerable if one detail went wrong.

Now Cucamongo was introducing Coco. It was time to go on, as in a play, entering from the wings, ducking under the dangling strands of rope, hearing the cheers from the rear of the house. Coco looked out at them and waved one clenched fist. His knuckles were calloused from soaking in brine, from constant use in training. He hauled off the sweater, and his warm brown skin gleamed in the light from the lamps. There were boos from down front, and Chino Cruz grinned, looming, a man big enough and strong enough to cause trouble without resorting to trickery. The referee announced the rules in an officious, stentorian voice, ". . . London Prize Ring and may the best man win . . ."

They had to pull off the coup. Then they had to get clear of the theater and back to the hotel. Then they had to collect from Cucamongo, facing down the deputies. O'Brien would be under terrific pressure to keep them off Buchanan's back during all this. It was the biggest headache he had toted around in a long while.

The referee was calling the men to tawline. Cruz was a head taller than Coco and looked in fine condition. He had the reach, and he would try to use it from the start. Coco would be tempted to duck under the extended left arm and go to work with body punches, then hard swings to the head, combinations of blows he had learned over the years. No one had ever defeated Coco Bean in the ring. Tonight could be a first if anything went wrong, Buchanan thought, crossing his fingers, then rapping the ring-post for luck.

O'Brien almost knocked over the water bucket. Buchanan steadied him with a hand on his shoulder. Coco came back and winked.

"That referee man, he don't like me. Warned me about everything in the book and some I never heard of. Never did say nothin' to Chino."

"Box him, will you?" asked Buchanan. "Box him and watch for the hand on your head pushin' you against the ropes."

"Like you said so many times?" Coco cocked his head to one side. He was not above making fun, especially in a tight spot. Indeed, there were times when this relieved the tension. This was not one of them. Buchanan did not smile.

O'Brien said, "Can't we get on with it?"

The man was strung too tight, Buchanan thought. O'Brien was not afraid, he was just plain nervous. He was not to be criticized; there was much at stake, and he was probably a bit hung over from prolonged drinking. Still, it was an added burden. Everything had to be timed out: the exit from the theater, the dash across the alley, the entrance into Cucamongo's office to collect the gambling bets.

The crowd was getting impatient. The referee beckoned for the fighters to come to midring. Chino Cruz moved like a huge puma. Coco seemed squat and overmatched as they came to the mark. The bell sounded. Buchanan and

O'Brien squatted beneath the loose ropes in the corner, each with his uneasy thoughts.

The tactics of the big Chino were immediately apparent. He extended his long left arm and placed it on Coco's round head. He moved his feet, walking around as a cooper walks around a barrel. Coco swayed, moving left, then right. The bigger man clung to his grip.

Buchanan called, "Get the forearm, Coco. Reach!"

Coco responded. He raised his right fist and chopped down. The knuckles connected with the forearm of Chino Cruz. The left hand lost its grip. Chino tried to back off.

Coco went down underneath and struck the body. He slung one, two, three, four into the middle. Chino started to fold like an empty sack.

The referee stepped in. He pushed Coco away. He said, "Now, now . . . give the man a chance."

O'Brien shouted, "Give him a chance? Get away from our fighter, you crooked bastard!"

The Mexicans in the back of the house were all on their feet, bellowing in rage. Buchanan did not take his eyes from Coco, saw the anger in the black man. He lifted a hand and nodded and Coco, all seriousness now, also nodded.

The referee got out of the way. Chino, somewhat bent at the waist, again tried to get his hand on Coco's head, shoving toward the side of the ring next to the canvas backdrop. Coco grabbed his wrist.

"Now!" said Buchanan.

Coco spun his man. He led with a straight left that sent Chino tottering backward in the direction in which he had been trying to force Coco. His head went against the canvas, pressing there, making a dent as Coco hit him again.

There was a dull thud recognizable only to those at ringside. The referee tried to jump in and separate the men. Coco bumped him, then stepped away, hands spread wide.

Chino came off the canvas as though shot from a cannon. His eyes were already glazed when Coco uppercut him. Buchanan nudged O'Brien.

"That's done it. Get ready to go."

Chino's feet came up as his body went down. His head struck the lower rope. He was not going to get up and fight any more. The referee counted so slowly that the Mexicans were yelling for his life's blood, but Chino did not respond.

Buchanan said to O'Brien, "Quick, now. Through the back door and across the alley."

In order to make the decision official, it was necessary for the referee to raise Coco's hand. He seemed reluctant to do so. Buchanan went into the ring and took hold of the front of his shirt.

"I'm a peaceable man," he said. "But I'm in a hurry. Do your job, man."

"Don't you tell me . . . "

Buchanan shook him. The man's teeth rattled, and his red face turned chalk white. "Uh, yes, sir . . . Lemme go."

Buchanan turned him loose. He was looking for Cucamongo, who had vanished from the theater. It was a bad sign. Hatfield had not appeared, nor any of the others.

The referee lifted Coco's right hand. The crowd was in an uproar, the Mexicans were moving down, fighting as they went, trying to get at their new hero.

Buchanan said, "Come on, make a run for it."

They went back stage. Still there was no opposition. Buchanan's hand was on his gun. They went to the rear door, which was across from the door of the hotel. O'Brien went through fast.

There was the flat sound of a shot. O'Brien took a step, astonished, his hands going to his left side. He turned and stared at Buchanan, then coughed and went down.

Buchanan's hand went to the butt of his gun. Before he could draw, he felt a terrible blow at his back. He stumbled forward, going down on one knee. He saw Cucamongo now, and he saw Hatfield. He choked out, "Run, Coco, run like hell!"

Coco ran back into the theater. He knew what Buchanan meant; their rapport was such that he did not pause for an instant. There were guns before and aft, and he would be next, helpless, downed. It was his job to get away and act later, when a plan could be made. If Buchanan died of the wound, there would be vengeance. If he survived, there would be a chance to rescue him.

Buchanan braced himself on one elbow. He heard Cucamongo said, "No, don't kill him. Get his gun. Fire another shot into O'Brien. We want Buchanan hanged."

It was then Buchanan saw the nun. She was huddled against the wall, unseen in the shadows by anyone else. Even as he tried to signal to her she turned and ran away.

Cucamongo was saying, "Take O'Brien's gun and ditch it. He was unarmed, get it? They quarreled over the bets —anything, there's time to make up a story. Come on, Hatfield, you know how to frame it."

"I know," said Hatfield. "Just keep the others in line. If you play the game, we've got him."

"We can get the nigger later," said Cucamongo. "He's got to be done away with."

"Sure," said Hatfield. "But Buchanan could die. He's hit hard in the back. I better put another in the front, hadn't I?"

"It don't matter. You saw him kill O'Brien, you shot him, but too late to prevent the murder," said Cucamongo. "It's better to disgrace him before he dies. Makes it better for all of us, him such a damn hero."

It was a neat frame-up, Buchanan thought. The shock

was wearing off, and the pain and loss of blood were taking their toll now. He had been wounded many times; he knew all the symptoms, and he was aware that this one was serious. He could not move in any direction, he could only lie and listen and try to remember later everything that was said and done.

They had barred each end of the alley, of course. They had moved astonishingly quickly on a plan that must have been preconceived. They had no intention, ever, of paying off a loss, and they had prepared for error, for the sure thing going wrong. Very clever; it proved that Cucamongo was smart indeed.

But Peter O'Brien was dead, and this made of Cucamongo and Hatfield and Dugan and Wilks murderers in the first degree. No matter how they framed it, no matter if they succeeded and Buchanan was disgraced and hanged, they were murderers. And, Buchanan had always believed, murder will out.

All he had was this belief, to which he was clinging when they moved him. His eyes blurred; then he remembered nothing more until he was stretched on a bed in a room with whitewashed walls and ceiling. The lean man known as Dr. Farrar was standing beside the bed, looking serious, looking glum.

Buchanan managed to speak. "It'll work out okay. . . . Just lemme get outa here."

"You are seriously wounded," said the doctor. "You are also under arrest. There are guards at the doors."

"Uh-huh. There would be. Look . . . you seen anything of the woman?"

"What woman?"

"Jenny O'Brien."

"I know nothing of a woman. You are not to be moved. I have orders from the police."

The man was trying to tell him something without putting it in words, Buchanan thought.

"You are accused of murder," Dr. Farrar went on. "This is very serious. But you are in no condition to be moved as yet."

Buchanan tried to raise his head. To his horror, he was unable to do so. He could move his left arm—but not his right arm or his right leg.

The doctor said, "You have been—we hope—temporarily paralyzed by a bullet that nicked your spine. I have extracted the lead. You must rest until you regain the use of your limbs."

"Uh-huh," Buchanan muttered. There was no use in speaking any further.

He had been wounded before, many times, but he had never been paralyzed. His mind would not fully encompass this situation. Danger from the accusation of murder, from the machinations of Big Jim Cucamongo, these were nothing. If he could not regain use of his limbs, nothing at all mattered.

The doctor leaned closer, as though to examine him. He whispered, "It's a dangerous spot. Tomás has been here. Mrs. O'Brien took the train to New York last night."

"Is that when it happened? Last night?" murmured Buchanan.

"Yes. Tomás has seen Coco Bean, who is safe. Your horse . . . Nightshade? . . . is safe with Tomás's people."

Buchanan asked, "Is there any chance me gettin' up quick? Like tomorrow?"

"I'm afraid not." Dr. Farrar straightened and glanced at the door where two armed men lounged, polishing their badges: Dugan and Wilks on the job. "Just be calm and do not try to move. I will look in on you later."

He went away. A friend, Buchanan thought. And Tomás was faithful. And Coco was safe.

The woman. She was the only one who had seen it all. In her nun's garb, deep in the shadows, she had been unnoted by Cucamongo and his people. And she had gone across the country, three thousand miles away.

Of course Coco knew, but Coco was not an unbiased witness, and besides, Coco was black. No court would grant a black man the courtesy of believing his testimony, not in that time in that place.

Oh, there was a lot to think about. A plan had to be made. He had to get out of there and find his witness and bring her back to clear his name.

He had to move . . . and he could not move. He opened and closed the fingers of his right hand. It was a start.

He began to will the rest of his right side to life. He put everything else out of his mind. He concentrated with all his enormous will-power on fingers, toes, ankle, wrist, elbow, shoulder. He rolled a little on his hip and groaned.

The two guards came and stared down at him. He closed his eyes.

The high voice said, "They'll hang 'im if they have to drag him to the gallows."

"Sure they will," said the low voice. "Good thing if he don't get to use his hands again."

"Damn good," said the other. "If there was a way to make sure of that, we could fix him up right now."

"It'd be a pleasure. All the bets we had to pay off. Damn his soul to hell."

"Big Jim said not to. Said the trial would make him a killer, make us the real article law around here. Said it was worth more'n anything, get votes and all."

"If he says so."

"But I'd like to finish this one."

"Best not to touch him. That doctor, the nurse, always snoopin'. Best not to."

They went back to their post.

Buchanan lay quite still, concealing as best he could the movement of his hand beneath the sheet. The two were clowns; it would not take too much to fool them. Still, he was not fully in control of his head, he thought. There was pain and some vestige of shock. It would take time, as the doctor had said.

He did not have that much time. It occurred to him that he did not even know if it was now night or day. Determinedly he closed his eyes and sought sleep, healing sleep.

There was a meeting in the office of Big Jim Cucamongo. Not everyone was pleased.

Judge Carroll complained, "You might have fixed it so the referee would call a foul. Or something."

Durand said, "I been payin' off all day. Lost every dime I had saved."

Big Jim looked first at his bartender. "And if I catch you tappin' the till to make it up you'll be as dead as Peter O'Brien is right now. Get back to your work and stop snivelin'. I lost plenty myself."

The bartender left, smarting, unhappy. Cucamongo looked at Hatfield.

"You satisfied?"

"It cost me plenty. But I see your point. Buchanan's got to be destroyed. If you pulled a crooked stunt and the Mexicans and other people lost money—you'd have trouble, maybe, hangin' Buchanan."

"Still," whined the judge, "it took a lot of my savin's, too. I bet a heap on Chino."

Chino said from his corner, "Who slugged me? Hatfield did. That's who slugged me."

"So it was the wrong head." Cucamongo shrugged. "The way it looked, Coco was goin' to knock you out anyhow."

Cruz came up straight. "Never! Get him for me again, outdoors, anywheres. I'll murder the black bastard."

"Just be patient," Cucamongo bade him. "Hatfield, it's damn mysterious where he went, the black man. And the black horse. That horse was worth some money. After we hanged Buchanan, of course."

"I got men lookin'," said Hatfield. "I been every place, down in the Mex quarters perticular."

"We need the black man."

"Not for a witness."

"No. We could put him away safe for a time. Like he could disappear when Buchanan was jailed. Then we could handle him, match him with Chino, anybody comes along."

"First thing's to hang Buchanan."

Cucamongo said, "They say he's a crip. Maybe for good. So we'll have him lugged into court and get it over with fast. The newspaper's been great."

"You can thank me for that," said the judge. "My brother-in-law has a lot to say there."

"Okay, thanks." Cucamongo turned to his whisky. He did not consult with them about the woman. She had taken the night train, he knew that. She was gone East. Time enough to bring her back when Buchanan was kicked off. He would send Hatfield, maybe go along for the trip. Hatfield could track down anybody.

Excepting the blacks, the horse and the nigger. It was just a bit uneasy, knowing they'd escaped. . . . But what the hell, a horse and a black man, what harm? It would all work out nice and neat and quick—and it had to be quick. The coroner had acted, Buchanan was accused, the court would be in session tomorrow. It could be handled before Mayor Castellano returned from the North. There was nothing to worry about. He sipped the good whisky.

In the humble adobe house, the woman nursed a baby, and by the light of an oil lamp Tomás studied the daily newspaper. He was very proud of his ability to read enough English to make out the meaning of the printed words. He wished he could do as well in Spanish, but Dr.

Farrar, his mentor, could not help him there. He moved his lips, murmuring, "Thus Buchanan is shown to be . . . a backshooter and a crook. These frontier ruffians should know that their day is over, at least in the confines of our fair city of Los Angeles. It is to be hoped justice might be served at once. The heartless killer of Don Pedro O'Brien should be tried and executed within the next few days."

There was a knock on the door. Tomás opened it and peered out at two deputies, the light from the lamp catching their tin badges.

"Hey, you work at the hotel," said one. "You ain't seen the nigger and that black hoss, have you?"

"What would I be doing with such?" demanded Tomás.

The second deputy looked past him at the young woman, who covered herself and turned her face away. "That your squaw, Tomás? Some looker for a Mex, she is."

Tomás said, "Sí, señor," and gave a vague, foolish smile.

The two men laughed and turned away, calling back, "If you see either of them blacks, you better call us or the hotel. Big Jim wants 'em both."

Tomás closed the door and his face tightened, he spat Latin expletives swift as a jaybird's chatter. The girl smiled and nodded, covering the baby and putting it into a crib. Tomás put his arms around her and whispered promises that it would not always be thus, that some day they would be free, that men like Buchanan would come, that Mayor Castellano would triumph. She may not have believed him, being female, but she caressed him and assured him that his dream was correct.

He calmed down and went outdoors. The house was somewhat disproportioned when observed closely; it was deeper than was apparent. The rear door was wider and higher than would be expected. Tomás went to it and listened.

From within came a low, musical sound, "You just be still, here, you Nightshade. Tomás, he'll come and get us. Then we'll go and get Tom, you betcha on that. Whole town can't keep up us from gettin' Tom away nohow. . . ."

The Mexican youth reached beneath his shirt. He unbuckled the money belt and hauled it out. In the dark he could feel the bills rustling within it. There were a few gold coins, too, but he had not touched them, not one. They could have bought his family a new life, true. But they belonged to the man who had been kind to him, who had treated him like an equal. The temptation was there, no question about it. He had not told his wife how he had stolen the belt in the confusion of getting Buchanan to the hospital, sneaked it right under the nose of the excited Cucamongo and his deputies, a very neat feat indeed.

He tapped on the door, announced himself, then went in. He found and lit a lantern. Coco Bean and Nightshade were a bit cramped, being outsize. But Buchanan's saddle and gear and his saddlebags and rifle and ammunition were safe. Only his gunbelt and revolver were missing, evidence in the hands of the crooked authorities.

Tomás said, "Here. Take this. You will need it."

Coco stared. "Tom's belt? You got his money?"

"I got it."

"You're some kind of a man, you know that?" Coco buckled the belt around his waist. He was hugely excited. "We get Tom away and I'll carry him to where we got friends. Plenty friends."

"Then we will never see him again."

"Oho, don't you believe that. You think he gonna let them get away with this hooraw? You don't know Tom Buchanan!"

Tomás said, "I have heard the promises of many. . . .

But never mind. Let us talk about escape. There is a ship at San Pedro. It sails tomorrow."

"A ship?"

"Dr. Farrar tells me Buchanan keeps asking for the woman, Jenny O'Brien. She has gone to New York, the city. Dr. Farrar says this wound will need weeks to heal. On the ship is a doctor."

"This here ship goes to New York?"

"Around the Horn, they say. That is good, says the doctor. Buchanan could not travel across the Isthmus at this time."

"And I can take Nightshade north," Coco mused. "Oh, yes. I can get to San Francisco. We got friends there."

Tomás said, "That is what Dr. Farrar suggested."

"This doctor man, he's true?"

"He is our friend," said Tomás. "He is friend to Mayor Castellano, you see."

"Let's get started," Coco said. "Dark is the time to do a deed. People don't see me good in the dark." He paused. "You're comin' part way?"

"I am."

Coco took Buchanan's rifle from the scabbard attached to the saddle. He handed it over. "If this here is needed, you got to use it. I ain't no good with guns. Truth is, I'm plumb scared of 'em. Any shootin', you do it."

Tomás accepted the weapon. He said softly, "There are men in this town I would dearly love to have in the sight of this gun. Yes, I think we will start now. The wagon is ready, other friends have arranged for it. Slowly, in the night, we go our way. By the grace of God we will succeed."

"You talk different," said Coco. "You don't talk like at the hotel."

"Dr. Farrar and the nurses help those who desire help," said Tomás. "We wish to be ready when help comes."

"Let help come later," Coco said. "First we got to get

Tom Buchanan outa here before they put a rope around his neck."

The wagon pulled up at the hospital. It was drawn by two wiry mules, and on the seat was a hunched figure wearing a poncho against the night air. A horseman came slowly to the far side of the wagon, then past it to a hitching post. Coco got down from Buchanan's saddle.

There were vegetables in the wagon and much clean, fine-smelling straw. Tomás climbed from the seat with bent back, walking with a limp like an old man. Coco lounged behind him. A nurse opened the door to the hospital.

Tomás said, "The fresh vegetables, señorita."

"Oh, yes," she said. "Bring them right in."

Coco handed over a box containing tomatoes and grapes and apples. Tomás went into the hallway, then to the kitchen. Dr. Farrar was waiting for him.

"You must knock me out," said the doctor. "If I'm to be useful they must believe I was overcome. And tie up the nurse."

"It will be the most difficult part," said Tomás, knowing that it must be done. "Let us convince the guards first, please."

He doffed the poncho and his hat and put on a white apron. Coco came sidling into the kitchen through the rear door. The doctor acknowledged his presence, looking worried and a mite scared. Tomás beckoned. Coco went into the hall, walking lightly on his toes. Tomás went past the two guards at the door to the room in which Buchanan lay. Wilks and Dugan were weary and looked soporific from the long vigil, sitting with their legs sprawled.

Tomás came back, spinning, great satisfaction on his bright young features as he slugged Dugan from behind. Coco made two great leaps and got an arm around Wilks's neck.

In a moment, two deputies lay unconscious on the floor. In another moment, they were bound and gagged with a torn sheet. Dr. Farrar and the nurse brought a stretcher.

Coco looked down at Buchanan. The mark of pain was plain on the usually beaming features of his friend.

The doctor said, "He can't walk, you know. You'll have to carry him onto the boat. Here is a note to the captain and the doctor. They know me. You have money?"

"We got money," said Coco. "Just lemme get him outa here. Tomás?"

Buchanan opened his eyes as they put him on the stretcher. "Coco?"

"It's me. Just you keep quiet and grit your teeth some," said Coco. "We're takin' you outa here."

"You and who else?"

"Tomás, from the hotel," said Coco. "Now you be quiet, you hear?"

Buchanan said, "I'll do my best."

They got him on the stretcher. He was enormously heavy, so that Tomás had some trouble carrying his end. They moved swiftly through the hall and to the wagon. Buchanan made a small sound as they slid him onto the straw, then covered him with blankets and fresh straw, so that he could breathe but not be seen by a casual observer. Anyone more than casual, they planned, would be disposed of.

Tomás said, "Coco?"

"Yeah?"

"We must hit the good doctor. Would you . . . could you do this? I will tie up the nurse, my friend, my teacher."

Coco said, "I don't like it. But I can do it."

Farrar begged him, "Leave a bruise. It must be convincing, or my life will be in danger."

Coco said, "That's my line of work, doc," He doubled a fist. "You ready?"

"Ready."

"Then, 'scuse me, here it comes."

He shortened the punch but Dr. Farrar went down, his eyes crossed. The left side of the jaw began immediately to swell. Coco tied him up and gagged him, forcing himself to do a thorough job.

Tomás was waiting on the seat of the wagon. Coco mounted Nightshade. He was the only other person in the world who could so easily handle the big black horse. He fell in behind the wagon. San Pedro was thirty miles away.

The dark streets were deserted. Coco rode the tall black horse, maintaining a distance from the wagon, ignorant of the way they should go, trusting to Tomás. He was unarmed; he could not bring himself to carry a gun, he hated them. If anyone interfered with the wagon, he would have to ride up and do what was possible with his fists. Buchanan's money belt was snug around his waist. The responsibility was his; he had seen Buchanan hurt before, but never like this.

The ship and the long voyage around the Horn was a fine solution, he knew. Dr. Farrar was a savior. Tomás and the nurse and the doctor. . . . You could bet Tom Buchanan would come back to Los Angeles for several reasons. . . . Meantime, Coco would take a small stake from the belt and go north.

Suddenly, there were other wagons on the streets. They moved silently, each going its own way. The vegetable-peddlers were awake long before the dawn, picking up their wares for the day. Tomás had chosen the time shrewdly. Coco rode with more confidence.

It would be a long time for him, but he could make his way. He had done so before meeting Buchanan, and he could do it again. He wouldn't like it . . . but he could manage.

# Chapter 6

It was full wintertime in New York, and West Street was slushy and the cobblestones mushed by yesterday's snow and freeze. Dampness came in off the river, and Buchanan shivered, carrying his saddlebags and bedroll like an immigrant from Europe. Teams of horses breathed visibly in small clouds as they leaned against leather harness pulling drays loaded with merchandise from all corners of the world.

It was ten years since he had seen the big city. He recognized the sound and the heavy beat of life the moment his booted feet struck the cobblestones. When he was very young and Luke Short had been with him, they had ridden the wave of the metropolis, laughing and playing and defying the law and the elements.

Now he was gaunt and he walked heavily, carrying all his belongings. Even the money belt, loose around his waist, felt heavy. The long voyage around the tip of South America had been pleasant enough. The doctor had been competent. The wound had healed slowly, and it had been difficult to exercise enough to get back strength. He had lost a lot of weight, and his cheeks were hollow.

A voice chirped, "Carry yer baggage, cull? Smash yer luggage? Tote your bags?"

He looked down at an upturned face. Under a ragged cap there were bright blue eyes, an engaging grin, a slight smirk of sly knowledge. The overcoat was too short and too tight, the pants too long and wrinkled, and the shoes floppy and broken. The back was slightly hunched, the arms long, reaching for Buchanan's burden. The hands were large, strong, and surprisingly clean.

"I'd rather hang onto 'em," said Buchanan. "You can run faster'n me, and you may know this part of town better."

"Hey," said the light voice. "You ain't no rube, huh?"

"Been here before," Buchanan said. Something about the boy held him. "You from down here?"

"Five Points." He pronounced it "Pernts" but otherwise spoke clearly enough. "What you up to, cull?"

"Lookin' for somebody," said Buchanan, then was inspired to add, "You wanta get me a hansom?"

"Horse car'll getcha uptown for a nickel."

"Horse car don't run on West Street, does it?"

"Well, no." The blue eyes grew brighter. "I bet you're totin' a gun, too. I getcha now. A real Western guy. The coat fooled me a minute."

Buchanan was wearing a blue jacket he had bought from the biggest sailor on the ship. It went well with the watch cap, which was all he could find for head covering, but did not match the trousers and boots. "Got to find me a store, buy some duds. What's your name, son?"

"Muggsy Maguire. And I was raised in Hell's Kitchen. And all that. What's yours?" He walked at Buchanan's side, keeping pace without effort, a long-legged hunchback.

"Name's Buchanan. I mind Hell's Kitchen. Pretty rough neighborhood."

"I don't hang around no more'n I can help," said Muggsy. "You got the makin's on you?"

"I don't smoke—and that's a Western expression. How come?"

They were walking slowly. Muggsy suddenly darted forward and whistled, fingers in mouth, a piercing blast. A hansom cab made a U-turn and came around a corner. Muggsy grinned proudly at Buchanan. "Gotta know how."

"Uh-huh." He put his belongings in the cab. He took out a four-bit piece, flipped it into the air, watched Muggsy Maguire dexterously nab it. "Things change in ten years. Where's a decent place to stay at?"

"Crescent House," said Muggsy.

The jehu on the box of the hansom said scornfully, "They rob you blind."

"But nobody *steals* your money," retorted Muggsy. "You pays for what you get, sure. And it's quiet-like. Culls from the West like it quiet."

Buchanan said, "Okay. You come along and we'll see."

"It's uptown," warned the cabbie. "Cost you a dollar."

"Uh-huh," said Buchanan. "I'll pay a dollar."

Muggsy scrambled into the cab and looked out at the confusion of heavy traffic around them. "Ho! You know what?"

"What?"

"I done about ever'thing this old burg's got to offer. But it's the first time in one of these contraptions. It's like lookin' out a winder, ain't it?"

"Could be." Always concerned about youngsters, Buchanan was amused. "Luke used to call you kids 'street A-rabs.' You *have* got a home, then?"

"Nemmine that." The blue eyes narrowed. "What you got in your noggin, Buchanan?"

"Five Points ain't exactly Hell's Kitchen," he said. "If

I could find somebody halfway honest he might could help me find a lady."

"A lady?"

"A . . . ," he hesitated. "An actress? Singer? Performer?"

"That ain't no lady," said Muggsy. "That I might could help on. But not in these duds."

"Uh-huh," said Buchanan. He called to the driver. "Stop on Baxter Street, will you, please?"

Muggsy made a wry face. "You know too much already."

Baxter Street was famed for second-hand clothing emporiums. It was a busy thoroughfare. Proprietors lingered in doorways, darting out when they had chosen a likely customer. The hansom drew up, the driver turned up his nose. Even in wintertime there was a musty odor to Baxter Street.

They came in a bunch at sight of the hansom and the tall frame of Buchanan. They stopped dead when they saw the hunched, fierce-faced Muggsy. Only one, a determined little man, stubbornly sold his wares.

Muggsy reached around and touched his hump, snarling, "What you goin' to do about this, Jew?"

The little man refused to take offense. "My wife, she sews for me. In a half hour, sir, one half hour, we will fix the coat of your choice."

Muggsy growled, but Buchanan asked, "And the price?"

"Cheap enough. Cheap enough."

"Dress him up a bit," Buchanan said. "Not too much. Just . . . decent. And see if you've got a proper overcoat for me."

Muggsy stared, "You gonna buy here?"

Buchanan said, "Look at it this way: A couple of gents goin' around in brand new clothin', askin' questions and all, people might notice."

The youngster shook his head. "I'll be blowed. A

geezer from out West and he comes on with the con over me. I'll be double blowed."

They turned to the wares the eager merchant was urging on them. Buchanan bought a tailcoat and striped trousers, black walking boots, and a hard hat. They were garments that could have been worn by Luke Short, his gambler friend. Once they had belonged to a man of some means, he thought.

All was ready but Muggsy's coat, which the woman was still sewing. They walked down the street and found a café, new to Buchanan's experience, a short-order joint where a sandwich and coffee could be had. The food was good, Buchanan was always hungry now, seeking to regain his strength. It had been a long siege, and he was impatient. He must get back to Los Angeles—and with him he meant to have in tow the woman who alone could clear him.

Back at the tailor shop, the blue coat was ready for Muggsy as promised. Buchanan gave the merchant ten dollars, which he was assured more than paid for the purchases. They climbed back into the hansom wearing their new clothing.

"New duds, new people," Muggsy said. He had mooched Buchanan for a cigar at the lunch place, which he now wore stuck in the corner of his wide mouth. "Now what's this about lookin' for a frail?"

"Frail?"

"Skirt. Dame. Woman onna stage maybe."

The wind blew cold on Baxter Street, an enemy, Buchanan realized, threatening him with its damp discomfort. He wrapped the new coat about him.

"Yes. Name of Jenny O'Brien. Maybe. Dances. Sings. Beautiful."

"She any good at it?"

Buchanan hesitated. "I'm no judge. But I'd say she was. Got a big ambition for the stage."

Muggsy said, "I know somethin' . . . A bit. You want to go lookin' right now?"

"After I settle in."

Muggsy said frankly, "I got no place to stay. These duds, they'll look crummy if I sleep in a flophouse."

"You've got a room at the Crescent Hotel," Buchanan told him. "And you'll be paid for guidin' me."

"You connin' me, Buchanan? But no . . . it don't figure, you spendin' good coin on the duds."

"Let's say I'm gamblin' a little," Buchanan suggested.

"Yeah. Gamblin'." The boy from the streets of New York understood the term. He lay back in the hansom and puffed on the cigar.

Buchanan looked at the crowded streets. The jehu turned the hansom uptown on Broadway. The topography had changed since Buchanan had seen it last. People jammed the sidewalks. Three men walked abreast, creating an eddy of resentment as they proceeded downtown on the east side of the wide street. Buchanan leaned forward as the tallest turned and stared straight at him.

"What's the story, Buchanan?" demanded Muggsy, turning to follow Buchanan's disbelieving stare.

"Mark those three. And look out for them whilst you're with me," Buchanan told him. He was already unsnapping the buckles of his saddlebag. Then he remembered—his .45 was in the hands of the crooked Los Angeles police.

"You lookin' for a piece?" Muggsy reached inside his new cloak. He pulled out a nasty looking over-and-under derringer.

Buchanan said, "They saw me, all right. They're walking fast. They're looking for another cab." He lifted his voice. "Can you get some speed out of this nag. An extra dollar if you get us to the hotel and out of this wind in jig time."

"In ten minutes!" Muggsy called. "Put the whip to the nag, mister."

The horse did not have speed, but the driver knew his traffic. People in New York responded to the proffer of extra money, Buchanan had noted on his previous visit. The cab turned on a side street, then took another avenue northward.

"Seventh is okay," Muggsy said. "Less fast traffic. He knows the city."

Buchanan said, "Those three are bad medicine. Bad luck they saw me. But they would be lookin' for me downtown. They had to learn that I came by ship. They'd know the lady took the train, y' see. Their boss sorta runs Los Angeles."

"Like Tweed?"

"That's what he aims at. But the law got Tweed."

Muggsy grinned. "But there's still Tammany Hall."

"I heard about that. Crooked as a dog's hind leg."

"Powerful as an elephant in the circus."

"Uh-huh. That's what Cucamongo wants to set up in Los Angeles."

"Sure would like to see California," said Muggsy. "Sunshine and oranges and all. I read about it in the barber shop magazines."

The hansom turned on 30th Street. This was really uptown; trees grew in a row and the brick building was six stories high and spanking new. Buchanan paid off the driver, giving him an extra two dollars. The jehu was highly pleased and promised to look for two such fine fares again.

The lobby of the hotel was small. There was an elevator protected by an iron grill, and marble-type stairs led upward just in case they might be needed. The rooms were medium-sized; Buchanan had seen bigger and more luxurious in San Francisco. Muggsy, however, was delighted, fingering the clean sheets, testing the bed, peering into the bathroom, where there was a zinc-lined tub, a large cake of soap, and big, fuzzy towels.

Buchanan said, "I'm for a bath right now. Then we can start looking."

Muggsy said, "A hot bath," and went into the adjoining room, leaving the door open.

Buchanan shut the connecting door and locked it. He had to count his money, figure out costs of the rooms, how much time he had to find Jenny O'Brien before running out of cash. There was more than five hundred dollars in his poke. It was a lot of money, but at New York prices it might not be enough. He needed time. The only way to gain it was to buy it. He needed to regain his full strength. The bullet in his back had proved to be the most severe wound he had ever suffered.

He took his bath, laid out clean clothing, then lay down on the bed to marshal his thoughts. He had not been amazed to see Hatfield and the deputies under the circumstances. With any luck, he would not soon see them again among the million New Yorkers in this huge city.

On the other hand, if he did see them he must be prepared. This meant carrying a gun. He sighed at the thought. He was close to Coco Bean in this respect; he hated toting a gun in a city presupposed to be civilized. However, there was no choice, and he would have Muggsy point out a gunsmith.

He closed his eyes. Sleep was a healer, the doctor aboard ship had said. He would take a nap, he thought, before dinner and the beginning of his search for Jenny O'Brien.

And, until he did fall asleep, he would debate means of getting her to return with him to California.

He had one eye open when the door between the two rooms quietly opened. Locks evidently meant nothing to Muggsy Maguire. Buchanan pretended to snore.

Muggsy tiptoed, looking around, making sure in his

own mind that Buchanan was not conscious. He could have made a jest of it otherwise. He saw Buchanan's money belt and pounced. His long fingers swiftly went through the contents.

Then, as Buchanan peeped, he put it all back. He departed the room as silently as he had entered.

A cautious street boy, Buchanan thought. He did not steal from a benefactor—he merely wanted to know how far he could go, how much the traffic would bear. It proved he could trust Muggsy—about as far as he could throw a bull by the tail. Or . . . until the money ran out. Undismayed, he fell asleep smiling.

The wolf den was in the Bowery, disguised as a grocery store. Behind it, the wheels spun and the poker tables flourished and the swells mingled with the hoodlums. Anyone who showed the color of his stake was welcome to play. Chuck-a-luck and keno were favorites with those lacking a bundle.

Upstairs were rooms for rent to responsible crooks. Dugan and Wilks watched in admiration as Hatfield grasped a well-sharpened pencil and squared off before a pad of coarse-lined paper. The Pinkertons had required written reports and Hatfield was proud of his ability to concoct them. His tongue protruded as he worked.

"Mr. Cucamongo, Sir:

You were right about Buchanan. He is here. We seen him today but he was in a Hansome Cab and got away. You know how Big this City is. It maybe will take us some Time to find him. But we will Do So because I am the Best.

There is different gangs here. One is the White Rats which knows me. Of old. If you will send mony I can Buy information.

We have not seen nor heard of the woman O'Brien.

We are still lookin. When we Find her I got a trick or two will Bring her around without hurtin her like you said.

Send the mony quick and we will take care of Buchanan and bring the woman back to you like you want.

Things cost a lot here. We reely Need the Mony. Resp'fy,

Hatfield"

Dugan asked in his high voice, "Didja ask for money quick?"

Hatfield regarded him without pleasure.

Wilks said basso, "Course he did, dummy."

"I don't give a damn, but we oughta go downstairs and take what we need," Dugan insisted. "Them games is crooked."

Hatfield said disgustedly, "And they're run by the White Rats. With Tammany Hall behind them."

"Them names don't mean nothin' to me."

Hatfield said coldly, "Then you're crazy. And if you make one bad move in that gamblin' room, you'll answer to me. And you know the answer."

There was a small silence, then Wilks said, "He's right, Dugan. This ain't our burg. He's been here before, he knows the way around."

"I don't see how we can operate without money," Dugan said. "We might not find Buchanan or the woman for weeks."

Hatfield said, "There's other gamblin' houses. I'll find out which is not owned by the Rats."

Dugan brightened and said in an injured tone, "Why didn't you say that before?"

"Because I want you to learn that you do what I say," said Hatfield in his coldest tones. "This is my business, findin' people. I'm the very best in the world at it. And when I get 'em, they're nailed forever. Alive . . . or dead. The woman's gotta be alive. Buchanan should be alive, and I got a reg'lar warrant for him. But if he's dead it won't much matter, just because I got a true warrant. A fugitive murderer don't never bother anybody much."

"Takin' him across country in handcuffs would be somethin'," Dugan said. "Dead—he wouldn't be no trouble at all. And the woman would be easier."

"If we find 'em," added Wilks, "Hatfield'll know what to do. That's for sure."

Hatfield shrugged. No need to brag, he was the best. But a few things bothered him, starting back on the night they had framed Buchanan.

First, he had caught a glimpse of the woman, and her nun's disguise had not fooled him. He was certain she had been a witness to the whole affair.

Second, someone had stolen Buchanan's money belt— yet he had just seen the man in a hansom cab with a companion who did not look prosperous enough or old enough to be the one who paid the cost. Who had returned the belt to Buchanan?

Third, he had little confidence in his present aides. They could and would shoot. They were not cowards—or they would not be here with him. But Dugan was stupid and Wilks was far from brilliant. He would have to do the thinking for them all.

Fourth, the nigger fighter had got clean away. True, he had not collected his purse for winning the fight. But he had vanished with the big black horse. He could not have done this without help.

And that was fifth and last in his list of worrisome matters: Who was the opposition, who dared to buck Big Jim in Los Angeles . . . and what did it mean? A man had to look out  after himself and his future. What could it all mean?

He conveyed none of this to Dugan nor Wilks. They would not know the answers—and he did not want them straining their brains to think, such brains as they possessed. They knew little of his past and none of his dreams of the future. The difference between them was that he could dream, still, despite his previous experiences.

It bothered him about the woman. He would find Buchanan, his connections with the underground, such as the White Rats, would take care of that. Indeed, if he could find the woman, she would make a nice piece of bait for his mantrap. . . .

It was getting her across country that worried him. He could not understand Cucamongo's desire for her. Women were like horsecars, another would be along in a while. No woman on earth was worth complicating a man's life.

However, there was the future in California to consider. The affair when he was a Pinkerton had been unfortunate—he had been caught. Others had been equally guilty and more fortunate.

It was another mark against the man Buchanan that he knew of this happenstance. Hatfield meant to kill as many as possible who possessed that knowledge. Buchanan for the moment headed that list.

There was a knock on the door. The three men reacted from habit, each yanking out a gun. Hatfield motioned for silence, frowning, then called, "Who's there?"

"Better open up and see." It was a woman's voice, rough and nasal, a New York voice. "You wanta know somethin', I can tell you somethin'."

"Could be a fake," whispered Dugan.

Hatfield opened the door. The figure that strutted in was most imposing. She was tall, and her bosom was more than ample. On her head was a huge hat, the brim of which flopped over her right eye. Her gown was fitted, slung in at the waist, swelling over the hips, tapering in to a bell bottom that swept the unclean floor.

Hatfield asked, "Dolores?"

"That's m' name, dearie." She slurred her words, staring at them in turn from round, bright eyes. She wore rouge and powder and something dark around her eyes . . . kohl, it was called, Hatfield thought. He looked closer as was his suspicious habit and saw that the edges of the boa and the long parasol on which the lady leaned were soiled. Her heels were a bit turned over, also, and there was a bruise beneath the powder on her right cheek.

"You wanted to talk to me?"

"Reck'n I do. If what they say around is true."

"Knickerbockers?" It was a password among the White Rats.

"Knickerbockers," she replied. She haved a hand. "These jokers okay with you, Hatfield?"

"Okay. What you got?"

"Nay, friend." She extended a palm. "Coin of the realm, dearie. Half in advance, half if I'm right."

"The hell with that," said he.

She started to strut out, then hesitated. "Gal from California, ain't it? Dark complected. High-and-mighty airs? Thinks she's Sarah Bernhardt?"

Hatfield said, "Sounds like her. But I'd have to see."

"Fifty now, fifty later," said Dolores.

"Ten now," he snapped. "Forty later."

"You must be out of your mind." She lifted her chin, very haughty. Her neck was dirty.

Hatfield said, "You know somethin', I'll pay what it's worth. You don't, and you know what happens if you take my money."

She shuddered for a moment. Then she came back into the room. "Ten hard ones."

"Ten paper bills." He counted them out. She snatched at them, leaving no doubt of her need.

"Kiester and Bial's," she said. "The eatin' and boozin' joint."

"That's in Five Points territory," said Hatfield.

"How do you think I got this?" She put a finger on her bruise. "My gennelman friend caught me makin' an honest dollar over there. Y' know what I mean?"

"I can guess." Women again, he thought, what a pain in the butt.

"So Miss High and Mighty, she ain't recitin' Shakespeare. And she's callin' herself Dolly Madison."

"Dolly Madison." She'd been some kind of problem in the White House, Hatfield remembered. Another damn woman.

"You check it out. I'll be around tomorrow and pick up the rest of the dinero," she said. "Unless you wanta take me to supper or somethin'?" She rolled her eyes and undulated her wide hips.

Hatfield said, "Got a date, myself. See you tomorrow, then."

He ushered her out as quickly as possible. He glowered at the grinning deputies. "One of the Rats is her maque, you get it? She's a whore, and not even a clean whore."

"Clean enough for me," grumbled Dugan. "It's been so damn long. Big Jim better get that dough to us quick, or there's goin' to be trouble in this burg."

"You behave yourself," said Hatfield. "I'll borrow some. If we pick up on the woman, we'll just wait 'til Buchanan finds her. That's the thing to think on now. Never mind the whore."

"You never mind her. I can think and mind her too," said Dugan.

"Bullfeathers," said Hatfield. Kiester and Bial's was in enemy territory but not too deep inside the boundary. It was sometimes a meeting place for the chieftains of the rival street gangs. The first thing to do was to make sure this "Dolly Madison" was Jenny O'Brien. The next was to stir up the White Rats so that a foray could be made on Kiester and Bial's—no big problem, since the gangs were always willing to do war at the drop of a Cuban cheroot. It would be easy to manage. He had only to await the arrival of cash from Cucamongo. He quickly took up the letter and added a long postscript. News of the woman would force Big Jim to hustle, he thought, sneering.

Buchanan grew stronger as the weeks went by. Under the guidance of Muggsy, he toured the new New York, marveled at the Brooklyn Bridge, rode the two new elevated trains, ate in Delmonico's, saw the elephant at Coney Island, took a boat ride around the island. His money ran low, and he went with Muggsy to Barclay Street where Jake Hall ran an honest stud game.

Muggsy hovered, worried, knowing the exchequer was depleted, doubting Buchanan's ability to tilt with the famed New York gamblers. "These guys is moider, they con you, they's at it day and night, alla time, they don't do nothin' else," he pleaded.

Four hours later, he was plucking at Buchanan's sleeve, pleading with him. "You got enough a'ready. You're luck is bound t' change. Quit, Buchanan, quit while you're ahead."

"Like to give the gentlemen a chance," said Buchanan, looking around the table. Shrugs answered him. Nobody cared if he took a couple of thousand dollars away. Actually, money meant nothing to these gamblers. They were inveterate players, it was the game that counted. They were, in their way, true sportsmen.

Buchanan bade them adieu and cashed in his chips. Muggsy walked beside him along a crooked street in awe, the first time Buchanan had been aware of real respect from the young street Arab.

"You took 'em like Grant took Richmond!"

Buchanan said, "Our people was fightin' for Lee."

"Who cares, the war's over," said Muggsy. "I wasn't born that time. . . . Hey, we can go to Kiester and Bial's, huh? Eat and drink and see a show besides? Gals kickin' their legs, high-class stuff, too. Best around and it's Five Points grounds, too."

They had been to the place once when they were flush, but Buchanan had been conserving his money since then. It was getting deep into the winter now, with spring not far behind. Buchanan regarded his youthful mentor with new eyes, as though he had not really seen him before.

For the first time in months, he felt in full possession of his faculties. The bullet in his back had taken something from him, something he missed. He had dimly known this was so, and it occurred to him that he had indeed been lucky to find Muggsy Maguire down near the docks.

It was also true that Muggsy had acted, shrewdly, as a body servant. He had watched over Buchanan, always sympathetic, always doing his best to provide information about Jenny O'Brien, always on the lookout for Hatfield and his deputies. Buchanan had, he thought ashamedly, taken all this for granted.

Now he said, "It's about time we had some fun. Show the way, Muggsy, we'll eat, drink, and be merry."

The street gangs of New York, aligned with political figures, were powerful beyond belief, Buchanan had learned. The Five Pointers and the White Rats were about even in strength, each having its connections with Tammany Hall, which in turn ruled New York. Kiester and Bial's was owned by high-ups in the Five Points mob, to which Muggsy gave allegiance. It seemed a safe place to relax, now that Buchanan suddenly felt like a new man, fully recovered from his long siege. He stepped out in the brisk night air, following the stooped boy around the corner and up the dark street.

Not that Kiester and Bial's was a place for the swells. Most of the men with whom Buchanan had been playing poker that evening would not have been seen there. But it was a gutsy, lusty embellishment where beer and whisky flowed and the food was hearty, well cooked, and served by hustling waiters who sang as they swerved with trays balanced on upraised palms. And when the waiters were not entertaining, there was a small stage on which fair— well, nearly fair—damsels kicked and showed pretty legs, a scandal to some, the prime attraction for others. There was a lead singer, a soubrette, who was of necessity younger, more talented, and better looking than the others, and, if possible, even more undressed. Of course, the patronage was almost exclusively male.

They entered the hall, peering through clouds of cigar smoke at the crowd. The greeter-bouncer was a gorilla whose smile was as ugly as his grin.

Muggsy said, "Hiya Jack. We done bucked the tiger tonight and won. Give us a table down front, huh, cull?"

"You got it." He gave the high sign of the Five Point gang and led them to a place close to the stage. There was a stand with hooks, where they could hang their coats. Buchanan almost slipped the long-barreled Colts into his overcoat pocket, but desisted. The bouncer was whispering "We got the ear there's Rats around. You got me?"

"Gotcha," said Muggsy. "We're carryin pieces."

"Don't want no shootin'. Yuh could knock a few about, though, we'd take kindly to that."

"Don't worry about us," chortled Muggsy. "Let 'em come. Some new dame or somethin'?"

"Yeah, we got a new chantoozy."

"Not like the one I ast you about, you remember?"

"You said a dark dame. This one's yaller-haired. A pain in the butt, too. Thinks she's too good for a fella. She won't last long, I can tell yuh that."

"She any good?"

"She's got the gams, she can kick a balloon all t' hell, she sings pretty good. But otherwise, y' know, no dice. Nothin', not even for the bosses. She's gotta go."

"The Rats want her?"

"Just a story we heard, like a little boid whispered. Keep yer eye open, Muggsy, keep both of 'em open."

"You betcha my life." Muggsy took out a cigar and waved Buchanan to the seat facing the stage. He was always on his best manners when there were Five Pointers around, his biggest ambition being to rise within the ranks of the organization. His blue eyes sparkled, he was happy with his inside information, his acceptance as a hitter and a real member.

Buchanan said mildly, "We don't want to be in a gang war, you know. Nothin' to win."

"Got to go along with my friends," Muggsy protested. "Prob'ly won't be no trouble, though. Rats ain't about to come dingin' in here."

"Let's hope so." He ordered oysters, having become very fond of the Eastern variety. Roast beef would follow, and a pudding. The waiters sang, and the stage was empty. The customers concentrated on the great quantities of food that passed for late supper in New York.

Buchanan said, "You been a real good boy, Muggsy. I'm goin' to give you part of the winnings tonight. You don't have to work for me any longer if you don't want. I mean, you can get a start—I won a packet, you know. Couple of thousand, anyway."

Muggsy swallowed a giant oyster, washed it down with a draught of foaming beer, and said, "Gettin' rid of me, huh? Givin' up on the dame?"

"Just about. Truth is, I about had enough city livin'. This here's a great place to visit, but livin' here ain't so good."

"But you need that skirt to testify."

"I've got friends in San Francisco." But that was no good and he knew it. He scowled. "Well, I do want her. She saw it all. She's the only one."

"She'll turn up if it's stage business she wants." Muggsy was concerned. "Hate like hell to see you quit."

"The city's too big." He could not even find Hatfield and Dugan and Wilks. An encounter with them might clear the air. Big Jim had also wanted the woman . . . And that was a thought. If Hatfield and the deputies were still hanging around New York, they had every opportunity to come across Buchanan. He had been expecting them. He and Muggsy were ready for them. There might be some connection. . . .

The waiters stopped singing. Men turned their faces expectantly to the stage. The footlights were lighted by a boy performer who did flipflops and somersaults as he applied the flame to the gas jets. The beef arrived, and Buchanan cut a slice and bathed it in the gravy with the potatoes. The waiters turned the hanging gaslights low. The piano player and the fiddler soared into a bright tune of quickened tempo, and the drummer rolled his sticks.

Four girls in tights, big-bosomed and hefty, came tripping on stage. "Fine figures of women" they were called, and Muggsy stopped eating to join the audience in beating palms together in approval.

Then a woman sang from the wings. The song was lively, but it was not the usual barrel-house tune. She came on strutting, long legs slim and alluring. She wore a gown, the skirt of which was slit to the hips. She was blond, defiant, and handsome.

And she was Jenny O'Brien.

The sign read, "Miss Olive Delasandrio of Havana."

But it was still Jenny O'Brien, hair dyed, showing more of herself than Buchanan had ever seen, singing in the voice he remembered from the hacienda of the late Don Pedro O'Brien. She was defiant, prancing, graceful, forceful.

And the men in the audience paid no heed. They talked among themselves, choosing the stout girls who beamed and grinned in the chorus. Some waved or called endearing names to those whom they recognized.

Buchanan said, "Muggsy. Take this money." He thrust a wad of bills upon the lad. "I'm goin' backstage."

"That's the dame? Too skinny," said Muggsy. "Dyed her hair, changed her name, huh? This ain't no place for a classy skirt, you know that."

"It's a place for a classy bloodhound," said Buchanan. "I got me a big hunch. You better duck, Muggsy."

"Duck? My mother ain't no goose."

"You don't know Hatfield and his boys," said Buchanan. "Better you should get out of here. You did your job. You led me to her."

"Luck," Muggsy said, grinning. "So . . . let the luck run. This is our lucky day."

"Only up until now." Buchanan arose and put on his long coat and his hard hat. "You been real good, Muggsy."

The youth folded the money with care, tucked it into his inner jacket pocket without counting it, an unusual gesture on his part. "What you think you're gonna do?"

"Take her out of here."

"The alley?"

"There'll be some hard goin'," Buchanan admitted. "Way I see it, Hatfield and company's around there someplace."

"With some Rats," Muggsy agreed. "You heard it. They knew when we come in here. They always know."

"So. I got to take my chances. It's the time. Otherwise, Hatfield'll get her . . . and me."

"Yeah?" Muggsy sat quiet for a moment. Buchanan went to where the usual little set of steps led to the stage and crouched there in the rolling smoke and great indifference of the audience. Now he could see Jenny's face, see the anger and frustration as she sang and kicked her beautiful long legs to no response. And looking past her from his vantage point, he could see men struggling in the wings.

The White Rats had arrived, eager as always to upset

anyplace or anybody associated with the Five Points gang. Hatfield and the deputies were in the foreground. Brass knuckles flashed, but there was no sound of gunfire.

Now the ladies from the line became aware of what was going on backstage. Squealing, they ran off in the opposite direction from the conflict. Buchanan looked back at his table, Muggsy had gone.

But Muggsy's overcoat still hung on its hook. Buchanan went up two of the steps and leaned past the flickering footlights. The little band went on playing in the pit, but Jenny O'Brien was staring off at the melee. He called to her.

"Jenny! This way."

She swung her head around. She looked different with the blond hair, not so sure of herself but strong with anger against the world.

Buchanan said, "Hatfield's out there. I can get you out the front way."

She came closer and bent to glare at him. "You! What are you doing here?"

"Don't ask foolish questions," said Buchanan forcefully. "Just come on down here while there's time."

She hesitated. She looked at the wings where the fracas was going on. "Like this? In this weather?"

Buchanan said, "You want to go back to California with them? Or with me?"

"With neither of you," she flashed. "Damn you, each and every damn one of you!"

Buchanan sighed. He had been more or less expecting exactly this reaction from her. He jumped onto the stage. He seized her and clambered back down to the floor. A few drunks cheered.

Muggsy appeared, the heavy-set bouncer and several others close behind. All were adjusting knucks to their fists.

Muggsy said, "Take my coat. Get goin' for Jersey.

They might live through this. They won't look for you in Jersey."

Buchanan said, "You'll hear from me, pardner. Remember, that San Francisco number'll always get me."

He seized the long coat and wrapped it around Jenny O'Brien. Immediately she began to kick and swing her arms, as though smothered. Buchanan closed one arm around her as tight as a boa constrictor and held her helpless.

Suddenly, a shot rang out from the wings. Buchanan felt the little wind of death fly by his cheek. He pulled the Colt and aimed as best he could in the swirl of smoke and general confusion.

The sound of the double action .45 was like a clap of thunder. Men hit the floor, some dragging their lady friends down with them. Buchanan let go again, and a path was cleared for him all the way to the door.

Muggsy was yelling, "Up the Points! Kill the dirty Rats."

Ruffians appeared from everywhere, including the woodwork, it seemed, caps pulled to the side of their heads, blackjacks dangling, knucks gleaming, short guns crackling as the Five Points reinforcements charged up on the stage. The stout ladies of the chorus were screaming at the top of their lungs. Kiester and Bial, men of substance and influence, were in the street tootling silver whistles to summon the watch—and as many more Five Points people as could be gathered.

Down the street, a hansom cab came rattling. Muggsy was gesturing. Buchanan bore the struggling woman across the sidewalk. She fought every step of the way. Buchanan muscled her into the hansom and leaned out for one last word.

"Keep anything in the rooms," he called. "You'd better move out, though."

"Right y' are," shouted Muggsy. His blue eyes sparkled

in the gaslight. "And good luck to yuh with her. Ye'll need it!"

But Jenny had ceased struggling. She sat rigid in Buchanan's grasp, the collar of the cloak up around her face.

She said, "I have clothing on Blucher Street."

"Too bad," said Buchanan. "They'll have that place staked out."

"But I can't go anywhere in nothing but this outfit!"

"Newark," said Buchanan. "You can go to Newark. I have money to buy clothing for us both."

"There is no train west out of Newark."

"There's one to Philadelphia," he told her. "From there on, it depends."

"On what, pray?"

"On whether Hatfield and his two boys get onto our trail fast enough."

"You think they will?"

"Hatfield is the best in the business," Buchanan said.

"I won't go back to Los Angeles," she said coldly. "I admit Hatfield is a danger. Worse than you. Perhaps."

"Oh, Hatfield don't want you," Buchanan said lightly. "It's that sweet old Big Jim. He wants you back there. He wants me disgraced and dead. But you he wants for a bride."

She twisted in the seat alongside him. "Hatfield will chase you across country. You could let me go back to the city."

"First place," said Buchanan, "it's you I need to save me from Big Jim's schemin'. You saw what happened in the alley. You saw them kill Peter and shoot me."

"I thought you were dead."

"You didn't care. You took the train. You thought only about Jenny O'Brien, right?"

"With you both dead I wanted only to get away."

"But I'm alive. Peter is dead. And I intend stayin' alive

as long as the Lord obliges," he told her flatly, harshly. "And I got a certain reputation to maintain. And you're the lady can save me, given a couple other breaks."

"I want to stay in New York."

Buchanan said brutally, "Ha! New York wasn't treatin' you so great, now, was it? I mean, Kiester and Bial's ain't what you might call fancy. And they weren't even lookin' at you there, not that I saw. They liked the beef-trust dancin' behind you."

"Damn your soul," she whispered.

"Sure. But it's the truth. Looks like New York ain't ready for long, skinny legs."

"Damn you to hell."

"Uh-huh. Now me, I prefer long, skinny legs," he said. "You're much better off to get down to Pennsylvania with me and start the long trip across country one way or t'other. Because that's where we're goin', Jenny O'Brien. That's where we got to go."

"Never," she vowed. "You'll never make me do it."

Buchanan said, "Maybe I won't. But I'll let you in on somethin'. If I don't, one of us is goin' to wish we did."

She shook her shoulders, crossed her knees, and shrank down against the cushions of the hansom. The wind howled through the dark streets. The way to the ferry was long; it would be a cold trip across the river, but Buchanan felt warm enough.

At least he now had a better chance than before.

Dugan and Wilks were using a pair of the plump show-girls for shields, shooting at anyone who showed himself. Hatfield ran through the smoke and the noise. He caught a glimpse of Muggsy Maguire and tried to get at him, but someone hit him with a fist, driving him across the room.

Cursing, he shot the man nearest him. He fought his

way back to where Dugan and Wilks prepared to take flight.

He said, "He got away."

"He took the damn dame with him," said Dugan. "I seen him go out the door."

"Why didn't you kill the bastard?"

"I was aimin' to. A goddamn hunchback nearly did me in with a little bitty hideout gun."

"I want that humpback," said Hatfield. "Okay, let's get out of here."

They managed to slip among the battling gang members without attracting attention. At that moment, Muggsy was helping himself to an overcoat, one of the fallen White Rats seeming to be in no condition to need it that evening. He stayed in a corner, watching Hatfield and the deputies.

There was no use in following them, he thought. Buchanan had a head start, that was all that could be hoped for at this time. From Jersey, he could either get a train to Philly and another train west, or he could go cross-country.

He reached into his pocket and took out the money given him by Buchanan. He leafed through it, his blue eyes widening. It was more than a thousand dollars. He knew to the penny how much Buchanan had won at the poker table. Half of it was in his hands. He put it away.

The bouncer came over and asked, "You okay?"

"Lost my partner is all," said Muggsy.

"He got clean away."

"But they'll check with the cabby," Muggsy said. "Couldn't get any of them three, huh?"

"They managed to hide. Then when your big partner scrammed, they took off. If I see 'em around again, I'll holler for the boys."

"They won't be around," Muggsy said, sighing. "Say, you remember we talked about openin' a hall?"

"Uh-huh, sure, I remember. Like we need a thousand."

The bouncer laughed. "Where we goin' to get that kinda dough?"

Muggsy said, "Talk to the alderman. The Hall man. I got the money, all we need is the law."

"You kiddin'?"

Muggsy said, "My partner, he's some kind of a man. You and me, we can make it. IF Tammany says so. You do your part, I'll put up the cash."

The bouncer was a boyhood friend. He was a good fellow, honest enough, faithful to old ties and to the Five Points. But there'd never be another partner like Buchanan. Not never, he said, brooding, going into the night, shivering in the winter weather.

The horse's shod hoofs clopped on the paving as the hansom cab made its slow way uptown. The jehu nodded on the box. It had been a good night for him. The long trip down to the ferry had topped off a profitable evening. Now, both horse and driver wanted only to make their way to the stable and the warmth of home.

Three men stepped off the curb. The leader flourished a revolver and said, "Get down from there."

"I ain't got nothin'," the driver whined. "Nobody robs a poor man in this part of the city."

Hatfield said, "You got a fare from the people you took down to the ferry. A man told us about it."

"Just a couple dollars. You wouldn't take a couple dollars from a poor old man?"

Dugan and Wilks dragged him to the street and went through his pockets. Broadway was dark and deserted.

"Ten dollars. A big night," said Dugan, pocketing the money. "You want me to hit him a few?"

"The ferry, wasn't it? Big man and a woman?"

"Did I say it wasn't the ferry? I need that money to pay for the hire. I don't own the rig," pleaded the driver. "I got to pay the owner."

"Pay him outa tomorrow's take," said Dugan. "If you're alive tomorrow."

Hatfield demanded, "What ferry? What did you hear them talk about?"

"I was wearin' ear muffs." The man sniveled. "It's cold up there on the box. I didn't hear anything. They was arguin' is all I know. About goin' west or somethin'."

"Give him back half his money," Hatfield ordered.

"We need every two-bit piece," objected Dugan.

"Give him half." Hatfield addressed the driver again. "West? By way of Philadelphia, maybe?"

"That's the way they'd go, y' know. Trains from Philly run west." The jehu gratefully accepted the five dollars. "Can I go, now?"

"Go," said Hatfield. He was already concocting a telegram in his head. Now Cucamongo would have to send money. Now there would be a long chase. And even if Buchanan was not apprehended—or killed—there would be a need for Hatfield and the deputies in Los Angeles. Otherwise Big Jim might find himself just a name on a gravestone.

# Chapter 7

Time became kaleidoscopic to Buchanan; his life was a series of events related to places. He could not recall when things happened, only the places where they had happened.

It started in Newark. He had registered at the local hotel as "Mr. & Mrs. James Bean," much against the will of the Widow O'Brien. He had succeeded in getting her calmed down and into bed. He had wrapped himself in blankets and lay on the floor.

He awakened to find her sliding his money belt from around his waist. He seized her and spread her face downward over his knees and whacked her. He did not slap her hard enough to break the skin, but he managed, he felt, to leave bruises.

He said, "California. Los Angeles. A court of law. Get it in your head, lady."

"I'll kill you."

"You and a whole heap of other people," he told her. "All out to kill me. I'm a peaceable man, but you all are annoying me. Look at it this way—Hatfield knew where you were. He laid in wait in order to get us both. Would you rather be with those three?"

"I'd rather be with anyone in the world," she raged. She was careful how she got back into the bed, sparing contact between the hard hotel mattress and her behind.

The next morning, she was tractable while buying clothing right for traveling, smiling at the saleslady, answering to the name "Mrs. Bean."

In Philadelphia, Buchanan took two rooms and used another name, registering her as his niece, "Miss Alice Adams."

It was his training outdoors, his plainsmanship that woke him up this time. She had come through the connecting door of the two rooms, picked up his Colt, and was holding it at his head.

"I want every dime you've got," she said with passion. "Every cent. I'm going to strand you here, Big Western Hero. I'm going back to New York and live my own life."

He raised himself to a sitting position on the bed and nodded. "Okay. Go ahead. Shoot."

"You give me that money belt or I'll do it!"

"If you're goin' to shoot me, why should I hand over the money belt?" he demanded. "People hear the noise that gun makes you won't get far anyway. They'll want to know what for."

"I'll show them! This gun will get me out of here all right, don't you worry about that. Now hand over the money."

"Never did see a woman so crazy about money. Why didn't you just walk out and go back to New York?"

"Because you made sure I don't have the fare," she cried. "You're a brute, Buchanan, but I've got you now."

"Uh-huh," he said. "You got the gun. I'm waitin'."

She lifted the heavy Colt. She knew how to handle it, all right. She aimed it at his head. Her eyes flashed with fire, as usual. Her knuckle whitened on the trigger, and for a moment he felt once more the wingtip brush of the black angel.

Then she dropped the revolver on the bed. Her wide mouth went crooked, her slant-eyes were wet. "I hate you. But I can't kill you. Brutes like you, you can kill people. Heaven help me, I can't do it."

"Leave heaven out of it," he said, picking up the gun. "I keep tellin' you, we got to get to Los Angeles and make a lot of people admit I didn't kill Peter O'Brien."

"The hell with you and Los Angeles." She went through the door into her own room, tears streaming.

"It's me or Hatfield," he called softly after her. She didn't respond. Maybe she didn't care . . .

By devious routes, he conveyed her to Independence, Missouri, where once the wagon trains had gathered to ready the western-bound emigrants for the long trail-trip, almost two thousand miles to the Pacific Ocean. The town was quiet, practically a suburb of Kansas City, but there was still an aura of frontier boom and an occasional boat for the south going down the river to railhead or to the final destination in confluence with the Mississippi. There was also an occasional wagon train, a small one, going westward.

Buchanan inquired about a riverboat. There would be one along, he was told. He bought tickets.

He was returning to the hotel, where he had left a now rather subdued if disconsolate, Jenny, when three men came around a corner, walking abreast, engaged in deep conversation. Hatfield had again picked up the trail.

There was a convenient saloon, and Buchanan disappeared swiftly inside it. There was only one customer at the bar, Independence had long since ceased being a boom town. The bartender idly served a bottle of beer, and Buchanan faced the door as he drank.

It was no surprise. A man Buchanan's size accompanied by a young woman whose hair was blond at its ends and dark at the roots were bound to be remembered by anyone who bothered to look at them. Hatfield was truly a bloodhound, he had the pure instinct of the hunter.

It had long since occurred to Buchanan that if he could sit down and explain to Hatfield that they were all headed for Los Angeles, the situation could be resolved. They might pursue their own paths, arrive in California, and take it from there.

It had also occurred to him that in that case, Hatfield and the deputies would try to kill him and take the woman along to Big Jim Cucamongo.

He had considered another thought: to make a stand and shoot it out with the three of them. This thought came only when the feeling of being hunted obstructed his sensibility. He was big and strong and quick, but only an ambuscade could even the odds against three men. And he was never a man to bushwhack even his worst enemy.

He had explained all this to Jenny O'Brien, and, to give her credit, she had assimilated the ideas. She hated to admit it, would not talk about it, but she knew it was true. She had stopped trying to get back to New York for the moment. She was, of course, biding her time—there was never an easy moment where Jenny was concerned. It all combined to make Buchanan, an easygoing, natural man, as nervous as a cat on a hot tin roof. Being in the company of a temperamental young lady who professed to abhor him made things no better.

Hatfield and his men did not enter the saloon. Buchanan ordered a whiskey to go with the beer and tried to relax. His concentration had been so deep and heavy that he had not heard a word said by the other customer, who was mourning his luck to the barkeeper.

"Sure give a lot to be on that packet goin' south," he said, a young man with the South in his mouth. "Them sharpers knew more about cards 'en me, that's for sure."

"Broke you, did they?" The bartender looked at the

coin on the bar, then sharply at the young man.

"Jest about. And here I am with horses I can't sell and no money for tickets."

Buchanan shoved a dollar along the bar. "Have one on me, stranger. You said horses?"

"Two saddle animules and a pack horse," the young man sighed. "Ain't what they buyin' hereabouts no time. They buyin' big-foot drays."

"The horses any good?"

"Good enough." The young man's interest quickened. "My name's Johnny Lamar. Folks got a plantation and all. I been prospectin', found a trace, blew it all on a poker game. Barman, here, he knows me."

Buchanan said, "I'm gettin' an idea. Would you be interested in two tickets on the boat?"

"What I need two for?"

"Give you a hat and a coat to go with," said Buchanan. "Pay you extra if you can find a young lady on deck and manage to get near her and pretend to talk to her."

"You ain't funnin' me, are you, mister?" The young man scowled. "You're mighty big, but you ain't that big."

Buchanan said, "Drink up. Then come with me."

On the street he kept his eyes open for Hatfield as he told the young man what he had concocted and why, and handed over the pair of tickets. "Wouldn't want to be on the boat with those three, y' understand? If you could make yourself a wee bit taller, and since the sailin's at night anyhow, they might fall for it. And we'll head west on the old trail while you return to your plantation and your folks."

Johnny Lamar said, "They won't shoot me on suspicion?"

"They'll look first. They'd most likely try to dump me overboard and take the lady." Buchanan nodded, that would be their way. "But when they see it ain't me, they won't try anything."

"'Course, I carry a gun," mused Lamar. "Yeah. Well, let's eyeball the livestock, huh? See if you agree it's good enough to take you whereat you wanta be."

They came to a livery stable and there were only three saddle horses in the place. Wagonmasters wanted a different breed, as young Lamar had said. Buchanan looked at them, walked them in the yard, knelt to examine their feet, looked into their mouths. They were sound enough. The pack animal showed a few marks from unskilled roping, but was sturdy and evidently could be saddled in case of trouble.

Buchanan said, "I'll deal."

"The coat?"

"Sure. Try the hat."

They traded and the fit wasn't bad, a bit tight on Buchanan, a bit loose on Lamar, who was above average size when he stood erect. They could stuff the shoulders of the coat, Buchanan thought, and he would buy a fleece-lined short jacket in the morning. It was coming on springtime anyway; they had been a long time on the meandering road to Independence.

He said, "Better not wear the hat 'til you board the ship. No use takin' chances."

"Got me another," said Lamar, accepting the tickets from Buchanan, handing over bills of sale for the horses. "Sure wish yawl luck, you and the lady."

"We'll need it," said Buchanan. He watched the young man go whistling down the street. He found the owner of the livery and did some business with him, buying additional gear.

He went back to the street and headed for the hostelry where he had left Jenny. Once again, anxiety seized him. Would she still be there? Had she tried to run away again? Had she thought up something new? How would she react to the news of Hatfield and company and Buchanan's notion of getting away on horseback?

He knew that he would feel at home during the last leg of the trip for the first time since leaving O'Brien's hacienda in the San Fernando Valley. It had been artificial daily existence from then until now. He knew cities, he was not strange nor afraid in them, but he was an outdoors man, had been all his life. He knew the way across the plains, down the Santa Fe Trail to Arizona and thence to Los Angeles. Though preoccupied with doubts of the woman and embryonic plans for the journey ahead, Buchanan returned to caution as he approached the hotel. It was a rambling building, a bit shabby, reminiscent of the frontier town of the past, the jumping-off spot for the Forty-niners. He started to enter, then went around the back, reconnoitering. He returned to the front, but his sixth sense, the one that warned of danger, sent him back to the rear of the building.

The yard was deserted. Then, in another moment, the rear door banged open. Hatfield and the two deputies emerged, hustling a forlorn figure.

Jenny O'Brien wore a heavy veil that concealed the gag in her mouth. Her hands were tied before her, hidden in the folds of a voluminous dress from her wardrobe. They had forced her to don that dress, Buchanan knew. He could imagine what that deed had done to her enormous pride. He almost chuckled as he went into action.

He did not fire the revolver. He did not want the town upon them, and he did not want to answer questions. He came in upon them from the side, before they could get to their own weapons.

He laid the long barrel against heads. He was not at all particular which head. He kicked Hatfield away from Jenny as the other two went down. He followed through with a long, overhand punch. It caught the edge of Hatfield's jaw. The man hurtled headlong into the wall of the hotel.

The other two were crawling around on their hands and

knees. Buchanan slammed one into the other. Then an idea occurred to him, and he refrained from rendering them completely unconscious.

He said, careful to let them barely overhear, "Back upstairs, Jenny. We got to get to the boat before they catch up to us again. We'll leave here. . . . We'll. . . ." He stopped, dragging her into the hotel.

He got her up to the room. She was gurgling and snorting. He removed the gag.

She said, "You dog, you dirty dog, I nearly choked to death. Why didn't you untie me and let me at them?"

He took out his Barlow and slashed loose her wrists. "I thought I did pretty good as it is. They think we're going downriver. When they wake up they'll be lookin' for us at the dock."

"What's so great about that?" she demanded. "You should have killed them while you had the chance."

He sighed. "Uh-huh. What I should have done was turn you loose and given you my gun and let you do it."

She flushed and rubbed her chafed wrists. She said, "All right, you can't kill people just like that. We're still in trouble."

"Maybe not."

"They'll be on that boat."

"Uh-huh. But we won't."

"Then they won't board it, either."

Buchanan said, "Reckon they will. It'll be dark. Fella looks a bit like me will be goin' aboard. You and me will be long gone."

"How? Where?"

"On the trail," he said glowingly, beaming at her. "I got horses. We'll pick up supplies right now and take off for the Santa Fe Trail. Then we'll cut over to Tucson and take the stage to Los Angeles."

"Horses? You mean to *ride* all that distance?"

"Best way to travel."

She said, "Me? Me ride across the country?"

"Well, you can take the boat. Or stay here," he told her. "Or whatever. I'm ridin'."

"I won't do it!"

"I can't make you, much as I need you," he said. He looked her up and down. "I can't keep you in the saddle, watch you day and night. But on t'other hand, I ain't ever undressed you, made you wear what I wanted you to wear. I ain't ever put hands on you, now, have I?"

The flush turned to deep crimson. She whirled away from him. She went to the window. Her fists were clenched. "I could have killed them. I could have," she muttered.

"If you don't go with me, they'll get you. Hatfield is a mighty hunter—of people. Maybe I should've killed him. Maybe that would've solved everything so far as gettin' back to Los Angeles. It's not my style, is all."

"No," she said. She faced him. "Of course you're right. Damn it, you're always right."

"Not when I walked into that frame in the alley behind Cucamongo's theater," he said. "Not when I let Peter get murdered. From now on I got to be right. It's the only way to even things up."

She looked around the room. "What do we take with us?"

"Very little for a lady," he said gently. "And I don't have to tell you to wear them pants we bought for disguise. You know, the Levi's. That's what we'll be wearin' for some time to come."

"You don't have to tell me," she said bitterly. "You don't have to tell me how the seat is going to be worn through. And to think I never was on a horse 'til I married and went west to the hacienda."

"You'll be all right," he said. "If you put your mind to it, you can do almost anything."

"Thanks for nothing." But there was a tiny smile at

the corner of her mouth. "Now get out of here and let me get ready. Otherwise you'll blame me for holding up the journey."

He was glad to escape. It was the nicest she had ever been to him, even though she hadn't bothered to thank him for taking her away from Hatfield and the deputies.

He only hoped the dazed men had heard him plan to get to the boat. Hatfield was awful smart. But of course Hatfield had been out like a light and would have to take the word of the others.

If he did take their word.

And Hatfield would be off that boat at the next stop. He would know that Buchanan was going cross-country. It was merely a question of where and when their paths would cross again.

In Los Angeles, matters of great import moved in devious ways. Mayor Castellano welcomed newcomers in droves, especially those from below the border who came with full intention of becoming citizens, people of substance, poor people of good character. Of the latter, there were many more than of the former.

Big Jim Cucamongo had his eye on Anglo emigrants, most from the midwest and the north, a few from the still debilitated states of the Confederacy. The hotel and the theater were gathering places for the sporting set, for those who merely appreciated excitement and amusement. Durand the bartender had orders to set them up regularly on the house, "compliments of old Jim Cucamongo, friend of those who needed friends." Free dinners were delivered in wagons to the neighborhoods of the needy—excepting the barrio of the Latin population. Big Jim well knew there were no votes for him in that section of town.

And he was running for mayor come November.

Down in the Plaza, two men sat over black coffee in one of the sidewalk cafes. Mayor Castellano was short and slim, with a fierce mustache and Vandyke. Dr. Farrar, rumpled as usual, his hands stained with medications, was smoking a curved pipe.

"If the pigman wins, the city will be bankrupt and worse," said Castellano, who spoke always in strong language. "I wish I could believe all you and Tomás tell me about this Buchanan fellow."

"You heard about him up north, Roberto," said Farrar.

"I hear . . . I hear a lot. But to believe? If Buchanan returns, Judge Carroll and Cucamongo will have him hanged before he can do anything to help us."

"There's the lady," Farrar murmured. "We need her testimony."

"I have met the lady," Castellano reminded him. "Before she was widowed and afterward. She will not return."

"As you say," said Farrar patiently. "You don't know Buchanan."

"Pah! I know women. And I know we must work harder and harder to prevent Cucamongo from becoming mayor of Los Angeles."

"We are working. We are registering every Mexican-American who is eligible. And some, no doubt, who are not. We are teaching the brave ones what it is to patrol a voting booth, and that so doing may get them killed. We are doing what we can among the Anglos."

"Bless you. But it is not enough. We lack the funds to buy the votes that he will buy."

"Perhaps." Farrar puffed on his pipe and added, "I just hope Buchanan returns."

"To be tried for murder!"

"A trial I'd like to see and hear," said Farrar. "It won't go to its end, I feel. Cucamongo and Hatfield—if Hatfield also returns—won't be able to stand the gaff."

"You are an optimist, my good doctor. An incurable optimist. Very odd for a physician." But Castellano smiled. Only Doc Farrar gave him comfort these days.

In the hotel, Tomás accepted the telegram from the boy and signed for it. Avoiding the desk, he slipped into the kitchen. There was a steaming kettle on the stove, and he quickly had the flimsy yellow envelope open.

He read the message quickly, "Buchanan on way across country, woman with him will return railway cut off at Tucson. Will need funds Tucson. H."

Tomás put the message back into the envelope and held it over the fire to dry it. Buchanan had done it again. But Tucson . . . Something should be done about the threat to "cut off" at Tucson. He would have to get to Castellano and Dr. Farrar tonight.

He inspected the telegram and thought it was okay. Big Jim always ripped into them with such anger and frustration that he probably wouldn't notice anything wrong in any case. On the other hand, if Tomás was found out . . .

It was an intriguing game, and a man had to do what he thought best for himself, his family, and his home town. Tomás took the telegram to Cucamongo.

# Chapter 8

The night was all-encompassing, shutting out the world. There were no stars, no moon. The old Trail was now a half-mile wide and two feet deep. Too many had traversed it in the years since 1849. It was desolate, and Buchanan was not sorry to come to Bull River and the turnoff for the Santa Fe Trail and the southwest.

The woman had not complained. She sat the horse well, dressed in the Levi's and a man's shirt and coat, her hair streaming, a sombrero secured with a string beneath her chin. There was a rifle in a scabbard and ammunition in her pocket. Anyone might mistake her for a woman of the frontier.

Buchanan pulled aside to the running water. The pack animal immediately began to crop the grass that grew by virtue of the stream.

"We'll camp," he said. "Be dawn pretty soon. Most people comin' this way won't notice us."

She said, "I can't see very well, it's so dark."

"You get down. I'll manage." She must be stiff, her

rear end must hurt. He had to break her in gradually, or she would founder on him like a green horse fat on grain and ignorant of the road.

She said, "I can go on some more."

"Uh-huh." He knew enough about her now to make believe she was tough and strong. "But it's best to wait for daylight. Got to make sure of the trail, y' know."

She dismounted. Even in the dark he could detect that she was stiff and sore. The mauling by the deputies had contributed to her conditiion. She was trying to be game, and he was touched. He knew she was making it up to him for having slandered him with her sharp tongue.

He said gently, "I got a knack for doin' things in the dark. And I know the pack. We can make a fire, I do believe. They won't be that close on our trail."

"On our . . . " She stopped, started again. "You think maybe they didn't believe we went on the boat?"

"I don't know," he said carefully. "I believe we fooled 'em. But when you don't know . . . you don't bet."

She said, "You think there's a chance they'll chase us all the way across country?"

"There's always a chance Hatfield'll be close by." It was true, and he wanted her to know the dangers. "There's also a chance we'll run into renegade Indians, or white men, or a wagon train of rascals comin' or goin' from Santa Fe or Mexico. And later, there'll be pumas and one thing and another. I seen all these things, and there's ways to handle 'em."

"I'm ignorant."

"Well, you never been there." He was readying a fire from sticks he had collected, knowing through long experience where they would be alongside the stream. He decided hot coffee and some bacon and beans from the stores aboard the pack animal would make the night more cheerful for her. She was quick to learn, but she had to be led down the proper path. He had heard of handling women with kid gloves, but it had never been necessary until now.

At the first flickering of the flame, she went off toward the water and he remembered that women's ablutions were different and more important than men's and made a mental note to bear this in mind. The woman disliked him, which was natural enough, and he meant to do everything to smooth the journey. If she toughened to the saddle, they could get to California sometime in late spring, he surmised, always discounting unforeseen delays. It was time enough.

When she returned, the charcoal was glowing, little feathers showing that it had been dry twigs a short time before; the pot was slung above the heat, the pan was beginning to sizzle lightly, and the bean vessel was propped to one side. It was a slick job all the way, and he was justly proud of it, but she looked at it, compressed her lips and said nothing, sitting on the ground, her dancer's legs folded beneath her.

"Now, I know it ain't Delmonico's," he said. "But it's road fare. Try and eat it for strength, huh?"

"I can eat it." Her voice was determined.

"I'll try for some fresh meat when we hit the plains," he promised.

"Best we should get on. Hatfield will meet us somewhere along the way, won't he? I know he will, so don't try and make me feel good by denying it."

Buchanan said, "He will. I won't."

"It's better to know," she assured him. "I'm kind of mad about . . . about everything. You know? But it's best to know."

"Uh-huh. We'll leave the Santa Fe Trail and cut across toward Tucson. Avoid people and some desert thataway. Though there's no duckin' desert sooner or later."

She was sleepy, he saw. He talked a bit more about what was ahead of them, then arranged her blankets, showing her how to use the saddle for a pillow. She nodded and crawled into a heap, lying on her side. She had not complained, and he thought more kindly of her as he banked the fire, leaving the coffee pot on, wondering if she could endure the black stuff in the morning, when he most enjoyed it and its eye-opening effect.

Only then did he realize with utter astonishment that he was dead weary. He lay in his blankets and marveled. The wound had nicked his spine, he knew. The long convalescence and the lack of outdoor exercise since had taken its toll. He was growing old, he reckoned, groaning beneath his breath, unwilling to let the woman know of any touch of weakness.

Yet he was only in his mid-thirties. He had seen it all, up and down and across the country, and it had altered beneath his roving feet, but he was still a young man. Not old enough to settle down at any rate, he told himself grumpily. He fell asleep, and for once a scowl creased his countenance.

When he awakened, he was completely aware of danger. There were now stars in the sky, and by narrowing his lids he could, after a moment, make out the movements of invaders. There were two or three men, who were silently checking the three horses and the woman. They had removed his .45 from beneath the saddle.

Old, he thought, and foolish not to set a guard. But not *that* foolish. He slowly eased his hand to his side, where he had concealed the smaller pistol bought in transit.

The three shadowy figures resolved themselves into a giant black, a sleek Mexican in a bolero jacket, and a slope-shouldered youngster. The Mexican reached for Jenny.

Buchanan said, "Wouldn't do that if I was you."

They spun around, and the youth went for a gun. Buchanan shot him.

Jenny came awake, springing from the blankets; in her hands was the rifle that had been her bed companion. The Negro made a swipe at the weapon.

Buchanan shot the Negro through the right arm. It was tricky in the dark, and he was very grateful for the stars. The Mexican turned, and Buchanan sat up. The Mexican's arms were raised.

Buchanan said, "Mind kickin' up the fire? I like to see who's attackin' me."

The Mexican obeyed. The Negro held his arm. The young gunner lay quite still. Flames slowly flickered.

"Thought all the bandits were long gone," Buchanan said. "Just chuck the guns down on the blankets, there. Make sure you ditch all of 'em."

He recognized his own Colt; it was newer and shinier than the one that was still in Los Angeles and that he prized. There was a derringer and a couple of nondescript revolvers. The Mexican had a knife, of course, but it wasn't worth quibbling about, since the young thief was possibly in bad condition. Buchanan arose and peered at the two men still on their feet. Jenny was holding steady with the rifle, and he was careful not to get between her and the invaders.

He said in Spanish, "You desire to check the health of your friend?"

The Mexican showed white teeth. "It is of no matter."

"Uh-huh," said Buchanan. "Just trail tramps, are you? Then git."

The Mexican laughed, shrugged, and started to leave. Buchanan reached out and caught him by the shoulder. The knife appeared, shiny in the light of stars and the fire.

Buchanan kicked the Mexican in the crotch. Before the complete effect could register, he struck him on the jaw with his fist. The man flew backward, losing the blade and going into a somersault, then flattening on the bank of the babbling stream near which they had camped.

Buchanan looked at the Negro, who was holding his arm and not making a move. "You want to stick around with 'em?"

"Not if you're gonna stay around here."

Buchanan said, "I'm sorry, Jenny, but we'll have to move on. Either that one's dead or he ain't. Whichever way, we're not taking care of him. And we need sleep sooner or later." He looked again at the black man. "If you people come after us, I'll kill all of you, Understand?"

"I already got that figured out," said the Negro. "You just amble along, mister. You won't never hear from me again. If I know it, I won't be in the same territory with you. Mebbe not the same country."

Buchanan said, "Be that as it may." It was a task to saddle up and repack the third horse and start southward and westward along the old trail. But it had to be done.

Jenny did not utter a word. She mounted her horse, wincing but settled down into the saddle like a Westerner, as she had learned when she lived at the hacienda. She had the muscles of a dancer, supple and durable, and now she saw the necessity of what they were doing.

There were worse people to take along, Buchanan thought. When they were riding out of sight and hearing of the thieves, he said, "You're brave, Jenny. Real brave."

"I was scared to death." Her voice was shaky. "I still am when I think about it."

"Don't think." He struggled, then said, "It was my fault for not standin' guard."

"Out there, miles from anywhere, off the Trail, even?" She shook her head. "It was just bad luck they stumbled onto us, you know that."

"Uh-huh. Could be. Let's hope we have better luck from now on."

She said, "You woke up in time. It's enough."

He did not ask her what she meant and what was

enough. He felt guilty still. He wondered if he had killed the young man. He thought he had. When someone went for a gun, you instinctively shot to kill, he knew. Otherwise you did not survive in the West.

He hated to kill without good reason. If he had been wider awake, or it had been daylight, maybe it wouldn't have happened that way. He wished it could have been otherwise. He hoped the young fellow wasn't dead . . .

When they awakened next time, it was atop a hill, a small rise but safer than the brookside camp. The woman stared at Buchanan from the blankets, then closed her eyes again. She seldom smiled and never laughed, he had found. He could see the dark circles beneath her eyes, and knew that the ride through the night added to all the excitement of Independence had truly taken its toll.

He donned his boots and moved silently at the tasks of breakfast, attending the horses, attending to every small detail in his thorough, experienced manner. After a while, he saw that she was really watching him through slitted lids, and, caught at it, she did smile. She stretched her arms, moaned, sat up, shifted her weight.

"How long?" she asked through a muffled yawn. "How long before I get used to that saddle?"

"Soon enough," he promised. "You got the seat. You don't bounce none like some ladies I seen."

She asked, "How many miles can we make a day?"

"Flat land, we might do fifty, sixty, even with the pack horse. Between that and thirty."

She was silent, figuring. "Yes, it'll be warm weather when we get to Los Angeles."

"You ain't fightin' it any more?"

"One thing I learned," she replied. "When you can't whip it . . . relax and enjoy it."

"I'll do my best to get us there safe. I got to clear my name." He felt the need to explain. "I mean, a fella can't let a murder charge hang over him. It ain't decent."

"No. It's a bad thing. But I thought you were dead . . . Oh, let me be honest. I had the fare, and I wanted to go home worse than anything. And . . . home didn't want me all that much."

"Uh-huh." He did not pursue the subject.

She said, "I'll take that stuff you call coffee, that mud and water."

He handed her a tin cup. She stared at him. "They had me down at Kiester and Bial's. You never threw it up to me. You know I changed my name because it was a cheap joint, don't you?"

He nodded, drinking his coffee. "Uh-huh."

"Well, I'd have done better. I'd have shown them." She stopped. She nursed the tin cup. "Agh! Maybe I will and maybe I won't. But I'll go back and try. I've got to go back and try."

"Why, sure. Like I got to go back and try to show Los Angeles that I'm no murderer."

"Yes. I understand," she said. "Okay, I'm ready for the bacon and biscuits. I never thought I would be, but I am."

"Ridin' makes you hungry," he told her. "You'll be real hungry before we get to Los Angeles."

He had never spoken truer words. They forded rivers, they rode the plains, which seemed endless, they climbed the mountains. They avoided main trails as much as possible, heading always toward the southwest. When they needed provisions, it was Buchanan who went into town while Jenny sat with the loaded rifle across her lap.

She grew leaner and stronger, and her skin tanned like that of an Indian, copper-colored and shining with health. Never talkative, she grew more silent with each week, but not sullen, not resentful. She had accepted her lot and was making the best of it.

Buchanan never tanned. Freckles stood out like fly

specks, and his sandy hair grew long and unkempt. He shaved daily, but his scalplock would tempt a drunken Indian, he thought. When they came into New Mexico, he kept both eyes open for his old friends the Apaches, who had alternately befriended him and attempted to roast him over a slow fire. He regained his strength and as they came within the environs of Santa Rita, the copper town, his back was no longer aching. Just below lay Silver City, where he was well and favorably known.

"Had been well and favorably known," he amended to himself. They made camp beneath some piñons on a hillside.

Buchanan said, "It's safe here if you want to go in. Mebbe you'd like to buy some things?"

She smiled faintly. "I should've bought some things weeks ago. Funny I didn't think of it. This has been a journey, Buchanan. This has been a lesson in geography, zoology, and people-ology."

"It has, indeed. You've been great, Jenny. You've been as tough as a gal could be." It did not sound precisely correct, but she beamed as though he had bestowed roses upon her.

"It's a once in a lifetime thing. It's something we would never do again."

He said, "Uh-huh. That's for real true. Look, I may be able to pick off a deer while you're in town. So don't worry if I ain't here when you come back."

"I'll worry," she said grimly. "But I won't faint, I'll come looking for you."

He gave her money, a good deal more than she needed. "Funny how you never think of money on the trail," he said. "Happen to have plenty."

"You think you have plenty. What about lawyers in Los Angeles?" She was becoming practical now that they were nearing the end of the journey.

"You go on, now." He liked her better the other way,

silent, primitive, expert. She was a strange woman, and he still did not feel he could entirely trust her in Los Angeles. Until then, he believed, she would be okay. But back in the city—of that he was uncertain. People behaved differently in cities.

He picked up the trail of a buck, followed it over several knolls, came upon it as it posed upon a rise of ground against the evening sky. This was the high plains and the color was unbelievably beautiful. He lifted the rifle, then lowered it, watching the proud and graceful beast, drinking in the loveliness of the land.

Jenny would be bringing meat, such as it was, from town. He walked back, feeling larger than life and a million times happier than the day he had been shot in the back. Jenny was already at the campsite. She sat cross-legged like an Indian squaw, with her head down. He increased his pace, fearful that something had gone wrong.

She looked up at him. There were, finally, tears on her cheeks. She handed him a ragged piece of cardboard. There were tack holes in each corner. On it was a bad likeness of himself, of Buchanan.

Underneath the message was that he was wanted for "Murder in the First Degree."

He looked dully at it, then sat opposite her. "Know how you feel. It looks mighty brutal writ down like that."

"I tore it down," she said. "I couldn't bear to see it."

"Well, now." He felt awkward. "That's why we got to get back there, y' see? That's the reason."

"Yes. Now I know it here," she said, pressing a hand to her middle. "In the gut, I know it."

"Well, you're the one knows it ain't true."

"Yes," she said. "And I've been with you all the way across this big, beautiful damn country. Me, a city girl. And I learned. And it makes me sick to see this."

She tore it into pieces. She held it in her hand.

He said, "I'll start a fire. It makes me somewhat sick, too. Murder. It's a hard word in print."

"We'll show 'em," she promised. "We'll damn well show 'em, Buchanan. You just bet we will."

Then she went off to the nearby running brook, which Buchanan seemed always able to find for a good campsite. She stayed quite a while, long enough for him to cook the meat and potatoes she had brought from town.

When she returned, she was scrubbed clean and wore new jeans, a bit tight, boots with high riding heels, and a lady's shirt, a light wool; she looked a bit self-conscious but also a bit proud.

He said, "Why, you're some scrumptious. Makes me feel like an old alley bum."

"I was right proud of these duds. Then I saw that damn poster."

"Never mind it," he said. "Come and get it. Smell good?"

"We will show 'em, won't we? We'll rip that Cucamongo apart, him and his crooked judge."

"We're goin' to do it," he assured her. "Eat while it's hot. The duds sure look great on you."

She smiled a little and held out her plate. He always served her, and she was a finicky eater never dipping her fingers into the food. It was a revelation on the road, he thought, when the idea was to get the meal into you and go onward.

They had burned the dodger. But it was not the "Wanted for Murder" that had bothered Buchanan the most. It was the heavy black print that read "$1,000 Reward . . . DEAD OR ALIVE."

But the next morning his mind was again serene. He grinned at Jenny and said, "I got a friend down near Lordsburg. We can sell the horses and take the stage from there."

"You mean I can dress like a lady again?"

He looked hard at her. "You been a lady all the way cross-country. How you dress don't make no never mind."

She turned slightly pink, he thought, but in the sunrise in that brilliant country in springtime, reflecting from the Mogollons and turning everything beautiful, pink and violet were the dominating colors. He went at his job of saddling and packing.

The horses had stood up well, amazingly well considering the hazards of the trip. He would sell them reasonably and get what information he could from Zedediah Harper. Then would come the last leg of the journey, through Tucson to Los Angeles on the new railway.

If they survived, that is. He knew full well the danger that, by all odds, must lurk there. He had to protect Jenny. He had brought her this far and he must get her the full distance. If she had been a burden in the beginning, she had made up for it since. No one, man, woman, or child, could have behaved better, he thought.

They rode for Lordsburg.

A telegram went to Coco Bean in San Francisco. It would be the first word he had from Buchanan. He would at once begin the ride south on Nightshade—if he were not elsewhere engaged in a prizefight.

Zed Harper had paid full price for the horses and saddles. He had been friendly enough, but, on the other hand, he had often been friendlier. His wife had sniffed a lot, and Buchanan had no reason to believe she was suffering from a cold in the head. Some years ago, he had loaned these people enough money to stall off a grasping banker with a hot mortgage. Now Zedediah reluctantly drove them to Lordsburg and dropped them off at the general store and then had departed in haste, leaving them with their gear stacked on the walk.

Buchanan looked after him. Jenny went to a nearby

telegraph pole and ripped off a wanted poster and tore it to pieces.

Buchanan said, "This used to be my country. I figured us to be safe anywhere near Silver."

"We're both learning about people," she said sharply.

They took their bundles into the store. In that country at that time it was common practice to swap what an individual did not need for goods that were necessary for him at the moment. The proprietor of this store was a new man, name of Hans Schmidt. He had a corrugated forehead and suspicious small eyes. Buchanan watched Jenny advance on the formidable merchant. Her reticule was extremely heavy, and when she dropped it on the counter it clanked. The owner stared at her, at her haughty eyes and determined chin.

She reached inside the purse and yanked out a gun. It was one of the ones Buchanan had taken from the bandits on the Santa Fe Trail weeks and weeks before.

The proprietor leaped back, raising his hands. "Don't shoot, a'ready. Take all you want, but don't shoot."

Jenny said, "What will you pay for these?" She produced the other weapons including the Mexican's knife with its carved ivory haft.

"I . . . I give you good price." Hans was obviously upset.

Buchanan stayed out of it. She swapped everything they had with them for whatever she thought they needed. The shopkeeper never argued with her. He was stunned.

Buchanan, chuckling, followed Jenny's maneuvers with relish. She was wearing a long cloak over a dress she had somehow managed to acquire—probably from Mrs. Harper. There were moccasins on her slender feet, but she was obtaining dainty, graceful boots, allowing the merchant to admire her ankles as he brought them to her. Her dark skin and peculiar, slanted eyes made her stand out like a jewel in this humble setting.

He had never surveyed her in this fashion before. First, she had been Peter's sister-in-law, then a nuisance, then the witness he needed to clear himself of murder. Then she had been a problem, then a good companion. Always there had been a huge if invisible barrier between them.

Now he was not so sure. He had seen her scare Hans Schmidt, then charm him out of his wits. And he understood it, how it happened when she smiled and approved of Schmidt's taste.

He stayed in the background. It was a time to move in the shadows, even in this country, which he had considered his second home. There was no question about wearing his gunbelt beneath the New York clothing Jenny had pressed at the Harper ranch. He also carried the smaller weapon in a convenient pocket. It was the dangerous time when Hatfield and the deputies might appear at any moment.

Jenny had also retained a weapon, a derringer. It was a nasty little over-and-under .44 caliber, with no carrying power nor accuracy, but deadly at close range. She glanced at Buchanan now, winked one eye as Schmidt bustled to wait upon her. He nodded and gestured, then walked out and bought two tickets on the next stage to Tucson, a considerable journey for the following days, a trip bringing him nearer to Hatfield.

She would attract attention, he thought. Well, there was no use hiding or trying to become inconspicuous. Nobody overlooked Buchanan, and nobody would miss remembering the girl. It would be at Tucson, he thought. He really was looking forward to it, to meeting Hatfield again.

And he was Buchanan, the peaceable man.

"$1,000 . . . DEAD OR ALIVE." It burned in his brain.

The stage-driver was a middling man with a short, clipped beard. He looked at Buchanan, accepted the tickets, and walked around to the street side of the coach, beckoning.

Buchanan followed him, asking, "What is it, Dick?"

"You never did it," said he positively.

"Nope. I never did it," said Buchanan.

"The gal with you?"

"She is."

"People been talkin'." He waved an arm. "You know."

"I know."

"Hatfield's been spreadin' all kinds of talk."

"Uh-huh."

The driver said, "If there's anything I can do."

"How many passengers?"

"Three. A preacher, a drummer, and Miz Jackson, she gets off at the way station."

"Apache Station?"

"Right. None of 'em will know anything about yawl."

"Thanks," said Buchanan. "You got a shotgun ridin'?"

"Naw, there's been no trouble lately. They never put a shotgun on until there's been a holdup or a killin' or an Apache uprisin'."

"Uh-huh. That's the way it is. Mind if I ride the box?"

"Be damn glad to have you."

"Be better for the lady," Buchanan explained. "Can't tell what might turn up on the trip. Better she should be on her own, like."

"Right," said Dick. His last name was Martin, and he had been up and down the frontier driving six-hitch stages for years.

"Play it that way. I'll be obliged." Buchanan walked back to the hotel. Jenny was waiting with two new valises, smiling and happy, a woman who had made a good bargain.

Buchanan said, "I'll get my gear. From now on we scarcely know each other. It'll be best that way."

"I see. You're disowning me."

"Uh-huh. For your own good." He felt much better. Dick Martin believed in him. Jenny was happy. The sun shone. Somewhere ahead lay trouble, but right now it wasn't so dark and gloomy as it had been.

He followed Jenny to the stagecoach, carrying one of her bags, his saddlebags over his shoulder and his rifle in hand. He helped Martin with the luggage of the other passengers. Because they thought of him as the employee riding shotgun, they scarcely noticed him after the first stare caused by his size. Jenny demurely got into the coach with the drummer, the preacher, and Mrs. Jackson, three people of no particular characteristics, going their way, anticipating a rough ride up and down hill to Apache Station, never comfortable in any stage.

Buchanan carried his rifle up onto the box. He sighed with pleasure. The air was clear and crisp, the road lay ahead. Dick Martin picked up the ribbons and clucked to the horses, and they were off in a cloud of dust.

Apache Station was just over the hill. It was sundown, and the shadows were playing tricks along the roadside and Buchanan was feeling hungrier than usual. The driver began braking as they came down the slope for the overnight stop. They were in Arizona, now. Buchanan thought of swinging down and walking the last half-mile, but they were already within view of the station. It was a low-lying building with wings for sleeping rooms, a corral where the extra horses were kept, and a red barn complete with chicken yard.

Martin pulled the stage in with the flourish no driver could resist. A boy hostler came running to take the horses, a man and woman came from the station to exchange greetings. Jenny and the passengers dismounted. Buchanan helped them, winking gravely at her and remaining to check everything with the driver, playing his part to the hilt.

"You want a job with the company?" Martin asked, grinning.

"With a murder charge hangin' over me, they wouldn't have me," Buchanan said.

They went indoors, where the table was laid and ready and the couple were bringing out food. A tureen of hot soup looked mighty good to Buchanan. He washed up and sat down at the foot of the table with Martin.

"Stage comin' from Tucson on time?" Martin asked.

"Seems if," nodded the station master. He was ginger-haired and his name was Hoffman. He and his wife were comparatively new to the country. "Rider came through. Said he seen 'em makin' good time."

"You'll be full up."

"We can handle it."

Buchanan ate. The food was plain, but better than at most way stations. The conversation was desultory; Jenny was silent. Buchanan thought about the stage from Tucson. When they had finished the meal, he slipped away and went outdoors. Night had fallen, and the countryside was peaceful and quiet. He took up a position near the barn and waited. He hoped Jenny would understand and not be nervous. She had her gun and possibly as much nerve as anyone, maybe too much, he ruminated.

The rumble of the Tucson stage became an echoing, faint vibration on the still air. Buchanan listened. If Hatfield was coming, he would not remain inside the coach, a target. He and the deputies were city folk, but they would chance a short walk. They would also be secretive, knowing that Arizona was Buchanan country. It had to be like that.

The vibrations ceased. The stage had paused along the road. Buchanan remained in the dark shadow cast by the barn, motionless. There was no better place to wait, he thought.

The stage started up again. In a few moments it had

come into the yard, and the Hoffmans were out to meet it. Two passengers dismounted, a man and a woman indistinguishable from where Buchanan stood. The boy was busy with the horses, and now Dick Martin came out to help and swap lies with the other driver.

"Three galoots got off up the road," said the man from Tucson. "Somebody build in there or somethin'?"

Martin said loudly, "I wouldn't know about that. Three of 'em you say?"

"Yeah. Silent jaspers, I calls 'em. Maybe we better keep an eye out for 'em. Maybe they're holdup guys."

Martin said, "I wouldn't be surprised. C'mon, let's feed them horses. The kid's overworked around here."

They came toward the barn, and now Buchanan moved. He melted into the darkness, seeking the large rocks, thousands of them, that were strewn beyond the station.

His eyes were already accustomed to the dark. He moved with care, pausing often to listen. Soon he could hear stones rolling beneath the town boots of the city fellows. Two tinhorns and a bloodhound, he thought, out to catch an old-timer in open country. It was laughable. He chose a boulder two feet taller than a man's head, clambered up on it and lay in wait. He did not bother to draw a gun.

He could hear their voices, now. They were arguing, Dugan and Wilks against Hatfield.

"I say we shoot him on sight," said the high voice.

"In front of witnesses?" demanded Hatfield.

"We got our badges."

"He won't draw on three of us with folks around."

The deep voice of Wilks said, "I ain't gonna get within arm's reach of that devil again, I promise you . . ."

At that moment they came beneath the boulder, nicely bunched, like kids walking past a graveyard after dark. Buchanan launched himself like a puma from his perch.

He landed upon them all spread out. He captured two

and rang their heads against the boulder. The third turned out to be Hatfield. The detective tried for his gun.

"Well, howdy. And thanks for tryin'," said Buchanan. He made his draw, the swift and lovely motion that was faster than the eye could follow.

Hatfield's gun was half out of his shoulder holster. Buchanan lashed out with the muzzle of the Colt. He struck for the jaw. Hatfield's revolver exploded once, then he was howling and spinning and floundering. Buchanan waited until he had fallen across his two unconscious deputies.

None stirred. He went to them and removed their weapons and struck them against stone, breaking the triggers and hammers as best he could manage. On each of them he found handcuffs. He pulled their hands behind them and clicked the manacles tight, pocketing the keys. He removed their badges. He sat down and contemplated his catch. Hatfield was bleeding a bit. The others were bruised. They would be conscious in a few moments, and he debated exactly how to address them. He decided he knew their thinking processes well enough to make his plan work.

He pinned Hatfield's badge, the gold one, to his shirt. The others he put into his pocket. He stirred Dugan and Wilks with his boot. They groaned, moving. They realized they were handcuffed and flopped around, managing finally to sit up against the boulder.

Buchanan addressed them. "Your mistake. You got within reach. Now you hear me. Right?"

They made scattered small sounds.

Buchanan said, "No, Hatfield ain't dead. Not yet. He won't be talkin' for a while, I reckon. But he's alive. Only he ain't the boss. I'm the boss, savvy?"

"Yeah," said Dugan. "I can see that. But what you goin' to do with us now that you got us?"

"You're not going to believe it," Buchanan said.

"You wouldn't just kill us and leave us out here for the buzzards?" Dugan's voice went higher than usual.

"I'm goin' to haul you back to Los Angeles."

There was a silence. Then Wilks said, "He's loco."

"You got to be lyin' to us," Dugan said.

"Back to Los Angeles. Just behave like prisoners and don't give me any trouble on the way," Buchanan advised. "When Hatfield wakes up, he'll agree. He may not be able to say it in so many words. I think his jaw is broken. But he won't want to argue about it."

Dugan said, "Crazy as a loon."

"You won't have no trouble with us. Not likely."

"Good. Ah, Mr. Hatfield's stirring there. Think you can walk back to the station, Mr. Hatfield?"

The detective's eyes blinked. He stared at his deputies, then back at Buchanan, taking it all in and comprehending the situation. He attempted to speak but spat blood instead.

"Got to get you to a dentist," said Buchanan. "Tucson, maybe, if you behave. Just remember I'm the law officer, and you're my prisoners. That way, we'll all get to Los Angeles."

"Batty as a bedbug," said Dugan. "Okay?"

Hatfield nodded. But his brain was working. Buchanan could see it work in the dark. There had to be a catch in it. Thing to do, Buchanan thought, was to keep them guessing, keep a watch on them, and make as much haste as possible. It was still a long way across a desert to where he must clear himself of murder.

When he had herded them back to the way station, he found Jenny walking up and down in the yard. She started and gasped when she saw the trio of handcuffed prisoners.

Buchanan said, loudly enough, "Figured they might be hangin' around here. Been expectin' to find 'em and take them in."

Now there was lantern light from the station and people huddling around. Buchanan explained that these were criminals, that he was a law officer. He did not say too much, assuming an air of authority. He would take the prisoners to Tucson tomorrow, he announced. One of them needed a doctor, he thought . . .

When they were alone, Jenny asked, "How are we going to manage all the way to Los Angeles?"

"Easy," Buchanan told her. "They want to go there. They'd rather I was dead, but this is second best. They think I'm plain out of my mind."

"Can you keep them manacled?"

"As much as need be," he told her. "When we get to Tucson, you can help. Until then, play it like it lays."

She said, "I see. In case someone asks questions."

"I fixed Hatfield so he can't talk. The other two are dumb as she-cows," Buchanan said. "I got the badges, that makes me the law. But warrants I haven't got. And Hatfield is well known and my picture is on them dodgers. So we got to move careful and quick.

Dick Martin was assuring the Hoffmans and the others. "I know Buchanan for years. He's been a lawman before now. Don't pay no attention to anything you hear t'otherwise. These three hombres are bad, bad medicine. They was goin' to hold up my stage, you can bet on it. Old trick, come in on one stage, hold up the t'other."

Buchanan whispered to Jenny, "People will believe what is told them flat out, you notice?"

"Even if it's a lie." She giggled.

"Sometimes I believe especial when it's a lie. If only it's told loud enough."

She said, "All the world's a stage. . . . Well, never mind that. I suppose you won't sleep tonight, guarding your prisoners."

He said harshly, "I'm a peaceable man. But those three,

they may not sleep. I aim to do right well in the same room with them."

He allowed them to be fed. He paid for the food, too, assuring the Hoffmans that he would collect from the State of California in due time. He examined Hatfield's jaw, did what he could to make the man comfortable. It was the way he was built, he couldn't help himself. Jenny concealed a smile, bidding him goodnight and going to her room.

But it would work, his plan. It had to work. He would chivvy his prisoners to Los Angeles and turn them over to the Castellano forces through Tomás and Dr. Farrar. He would force Cucamongo into court and, with Jenny as his witness would prove his innocence.

He lay awake a couple of hours, figuring it all out, planning each step. He would have no trouble getting to the California city with his charges, he knew that. They would not talk, they were as anxious as he to return to the scene of the crime. It was how he would proceed after arriving. It could wait. He took a last look at his uncomfortably trussed prisoners, and slept.

# Chapter 9

Big Jim Cucamongo poured whisky and stared across his office at Judge Carroll. "I'm payin' for it, you know. What the hell's wrong?"

The judge sipped his drink. "Er—well, I can only guess. The hotel, the theater. Er . . . certain happenstances. Dugan . . . Chino Cruz . . . Durand."

"The greasers hate 'em, sure. We can handle the greasers. Come election day their votes won't count."

Carroll shook his head. "It won't be that simple. Castellano is appealing to Sacramento. He'll get help at the polls."

"Damn it, you got to do somethin'. If we had that Buchanan and could hang him. . . . But there's no chance of that. I'd give a lot to know how he got clean away."

"It would help," said the judge drily. "There's a leak somewhere. Castellano knows what's happening all the time."

"You think I can't get elected?"

"Oh, you can get elected. We have roughnecks enough

147

to steal the election. But Castellano and the guards at the polls and a rather large element of people with money . . . they'll still be here."

"Damn them to the devil," said Cucamongo. "Lemme get in office and I'll go 'way past them. I'll go up and up. Once a man is in and got his organization. . . . Like Tammany in New York. It's a cinch."

"Buchanan would've given us a cause," said Carroll. "The new civilization against the old gun law. Too bad."

"The money I wasted on that damn Hatfield," mourned Cucamongo. "He must've taken off with the last of it."

There was a meek tap on the door leading to the alley behind the theater, startling the judge to his feet. Big Jim took a revolver from his drawer and bawled, "Who's there?"

The hoarse voice of Chino Cruz said, "Me, boss. Me. You better come look."

"Look at what?" He went grumbling to the door. The giant fighter stood his ground, beckoning.

"You better look is all."

Judge Carroll said, "Well, I'll be running along. Nice to talk to you, Jim."

"You get to work on them people," said he. Carroll would scuttle off if there was any trouble in prospect, that was his way. It kept him free of jail, at that. He stared at Chino. "Now, what's this? I hire you to guard us, not to interrupt."

The prizefighter said, "I heard you say you was mad at 'em, boss, is all. Look. There they are."

He turned a dark lantern upon the alley. Three bodies lay in a heap. Cucamongo stepped back, the revolver still clutched in his hand. Then he took a deep breath and demanded, "Who you talkin' about? Who is it?"

One of the men struggled and kicked his feet, which were bound with rope. Muffled sounds mewed on the night air.

Chino Cruz said, "Hey, they're alive. I thought they was all dead. It's Hatfield and them."

"Bring that lantern here." Cucamongo went to where the men lay. It was, he realized suddenly, just where Peter O'Brien and then Buchanan had fallen.

Chino asked, "You want me to scrag 'em, boss?"

"Scrag them? Certainly not. Bring them—bring them into my office."

He went ahead, locking the door to the barroom, moving furniture, spreading a horse blanket from the closet so that his carpet might not be dirtied. He sat in his chair and poured whiskey and drank it down while Chino carried in the three men and propped them, bound, gagged and handcuffed, against the wall.

"Take the gags out," Cucamongo ordered. "Let's hear what they got to say."

The big man went to Hatfield first, to be rewarded with a curse and a groan through clenched teeth. The detective's jaw was still swollen. The other two coughed and choked and looked wanly and bleary-eyed at the boss.

"Cheez, give us a drink," begged Dugan. "Hatfield, he can't hardly talk at all, his jaw's broke all to pieces."

"Get a bottle from the shelf, there," Cucamongo said, making certain it was not the good stuff. Chino poured the whiskey, then went to release the hands of the trio.

Dugan said, "That goddamn Buchanan took the keys. He used our own damn cuffs on us."

Chino went from one to the other, holding the drinks to their mouths. Hatfield drooled all over his soiled shirt. Dugan sputtered but gained some strength.

"Cheez, boss, what we been through. That sonofabitch jumped us outside this way station, see? He like to kill us. Then he cuffed us and brought us all the way here."

Wilks croaked, "Him and that gal."

"Girl? What girl?" demanded Cucamongo.

"The O'Brien wench you wanted us to bring to you,"

said Dugan. "She's with him. They blindfolded us and put us in a damn wagon and brought us here and dumped us off. I don't know how he done it, but he did. Him and her."

"Jenny O'Brien? She's in town?"

"Town I wouldn't know about. They move, them two. They been together all the way from New York," said Dugan with malice. "We overheard enough to know that."

"From New York? But . . . but . . ." He shut his mouth tight. He must not let these men know how he felt. They would consider it a sign of weakness. He waved a hand at Chino. "Get a file. First take the rope off their ankles. Then help them out of the handcuffs. I want to hear the whole story."

"It's some story, boss," said Dugan. "Poor Hatfield, there, he can talk a little. Get us somethin' to eat and some more booze, huh? It's some story, believe me."

"It had better be good," said Cucamongo. But there was no real blame to attach to them, he thought. They had tried. They had followed Buchanan, they had figured his destination, and they had intercepted him.

Or rather he had intercepted them. It was not that Hatfield and the deputies were wrong, it was just that Buchanan was always right. It was getting monotonous.

He said, "If Buchanan's back here, we've got to stick him in jail. The judge'll do the rest. So cheer up."

He caught the glare in Hatfield's eyes, and it made him feel good. The detective was enraged, and he would go after Buchanan with his dying breath. It would all work out. Buchanan was good, but he could not whip an organization like the one Big Jim had built. He helped the three men to whiskey himself this time, waiting for Chino to bring the file to cut away the manacles.

Buchanan drove the horse around to the rear entry of the hospital. The door, he knew well, was never locked.

Alongside him, Jenny O'Brien huddled in a bonnet and shawl, sagging a bit so that she appeared older and smaller. Buchanan wore a battered hat and a poncho that disguised him well enough for night, he thought. But his size might give him away to a knowledgeable beholder, and he was aware of Big Jim's spy system. Secrecy was important for now.

It was after midnight. Jenny scolded, "Now, scrooch down. Under the poncho it'll make you look shorter. Pull your head into your thick neck."

"You're the actress," he said, nettled. "This ain't my dish o' tea nohow."

"Just do as I say." She was crawling down from the wagon, appearing somewhat decrepit. It wasn't entirely the way she moved, he realized, it was an attitude. She believed she was an aging Mexican woman. He followed her, trying to obey her instructions. They went through the rear door; a nurse, male, dark-skinned, met them, eyebrows raised, asking if they needed medical attention.

"Just want to talk to Doc Farrar," gasped Buchanan, trying to talk falsetto. "Just wanta talk to him."

"Doctor's asleep. He needs every minute he can get." The young man was sleepy but stubborn.

Jenny pressed Buchanan's arm, clinging to him and murmured, "We can wait, darling."

Buchanan said, "Uh . . . yeah. My wife wants to see him. We'll wait."

"As you say." The youth went back to his cot and was immediately sound asleep.

Jenny said, "You know where he sleeps."

"Uh-huh." Buchanan led the way to the room behind the receiving office. Fumbling, he lit a lamp beside the bed of the sleeping Dr. Farrar.

The circles beneath his eyes told of Farrar's exhaustion. Buchanan hated to waken him, but time was of the essence. Even the youthful attendant might be in the employ of Cucamongo. He touched the doctor's arm and spoke in a whisper, "It's me, Doc. Me and Jenny."

The blue eyes opened. The lips curved in a tender smile. Farrar did not look at Buchanan. His gaze was on Jenny.

"I got your message." He sat up, fully clothed, but his shirt unbuttoned and his hair wild on his head. "I didn't expect you here tonight, though."

"The man didn't savvy too good," Buchanan told him. "Paid him to borrow the wagon. It's outside waitin' for him if he wants it for tomorrow's vegetables."

Farrar asked, "Are you all together, you two?" The smile lingered on Jenny. "Have you a plan?"

"Somewhat," Buchanan said. "We left Hatfield and his pals in the alley. Main thing is to make sure they don't shoot me for tryin' to escape or something. Jenny hides here, you bring her to court. If I can get to court."

"That's a problem." Farrar sobered. "Mayor Castellano is with us—with anyone who's against Cucamongo. But he only knows you by reputation."

"Which reputation, here . . . or up north?"

"Fortunately; both. He desperately wants Cucamongo removed from politics. But he has no strength. My hospital is full of Mexican-Americans who tried to register, who were overheard saying anything against Big Jim. They're resting on my floor. It's a sad situation."

"The ranch?" asked Jenny.

"Cucamongo took it over, foreclosed the mortgage."

"But Peter bet him . . ." She stopped, shrugged. "They'd deny that, of course."

Farrar flushed. "I—uh—attempted to tell the court. But no one believed me. And you . . . you and Buchanan were gone."

She said quickly, "And that's when they began to suspect you? When you tried to help me?"

"Well, they were suspicious after Buchanan escaped,"

he said lamely. "Now they send the police around regularly."

Buchanan said, "I'll get out of here. Is Tomás still at the hotel?"

"He's the best spy we have."

"Okay. I'll go before they begin searching. Jenny—you can disguise yourself so they'll never know you, right?"

"I can." She looked at him soberly. "You know what?"

"What?" Buchanan was on his way to the door.

"I began by hating your guts. I fought. I struggled. You beat me every time. I hated you more. And now . . ." her voice lowered, softened. "When you told that boy you were my husband . . . I almost believed it."

Buchanan saw the stricken expression that crossed the face of the young doctor. He said hastily, "You'll get over that feelin', ma'am. Now, take care of each other, you hear me? I'll get word to you when I know somethin'."

He left. He walked out into the street, wearing his gun belt and a holdout gun, a poncho and a Spanish sombrero. He tried to walk as Jenny had dictated, hunched over. He essayed a limp. It was very difficult to keep all this in mind as he made his way toward the hotel owned by Big Jim Cucamongo.

He lurched around and to the stable where he had first left Nightshade, and came upon the hostler. As he entered there was a noisy nickering and a big, black horse reared in his stall. The boy appeared, eyes big and round.

Buchanan said, "All right, I'm here, I'm here," and went to the horse. "Where are you, Coco?"

Coco Bean roused himself from a bale of hay. He rubbed his eyes and said, "Just got here. I been worried. Reckon they wouldn't of liked to see me in their barn."

Buchanan asked the boy, "Tomás in the hotel?"

"Sí, señor. I told him about Señor Coco."

"Tell him about me," said Buchanan. "And make it

quick, because I got a notion we'll all be in trouble before morning."

He put an arm around Coco's shoulder. The prize-fighter said, "It's been a long time. Had three fights up around San Francisco. People talked. About Los Angeles and how bad it is down here. They figure you didn't murder anybody. But they also figure you'll prove it. Know what I mean?"

Buchanan said sadly, "Sure. Even my friends who know I'm a peaceable man."

"Right," said Coco. "People is peculiar, like you always tell me."

"Got to clear myself," said Buchanan. "All legal. Got to convene a court."

"Whatever that means, you got to do it, all right," Coco said.

"And right now," added Buchanan. "Before they find you and Nightshade . . . although this is the last place they'd look, I reckon."

Footsteps approached, and he heard Tomás's voice, "It is I, Señor Buchanan. And you have returned."

"What's the situation?" Buchanan shook hands with the bellman of the hotel. "We've got to move fast."

"The mayor. You must see Castellano."

"He can't convene the court," said Buchanan. "Not his job."

"But he can give help. Judge Carroll is your man. How can you handle him without surrendering? And you must not allow them to jail you. They will kill you."

"I know," said Buchanan. "I've thought about it. We just got to get Carroll and speak with him."

"They may find you before you can do that."

"In that case . . . I'll surrender."

"And be murdered?"

"I could take Coco here, and maybe some people you could get, and I could go out there and start fightin'," he said. "A lot of people would get hurt and what would we prove?"

"If we could get rid of Cucamongo," Tomás said.

"Not enough. No, it's got to be a court. Some kind of a court. And a newspaper reporter to tell about it so nobody will be in any doubt. And a jury to decide who's tellin' the truth, us or them."

"Mayor Castellano can help," Tomás said. "Judge Carroll—he will be at the hotel. I will speak with him. We have an organization, señors. We follow and watch. But the courthouse? I do not know."

"How about the theater?" asked Buchanan. "Where they tried to bust Coco with a club? Where it started, that night."

"The theater?" Tomás considered. "Why not?"

"The mayor first, then?"

Tomás said, "Our mayor, he is a fine man. Very serious. The best we have." His eyes twinkled. "Also dramatic. A night trial. A judge forced to sit in court. A jury from the people. And all in a theater. He will like that."

"Let's get to him. Coco, you better stay here. Keep your head down and watch over Nightshade. Okay?"

"The hostler is loyal," said Tomás. "He will help."

"If he'll bring somethin' to eat and lemme sleep a while," Coco suggested.

"He'll do as you ask."

"You need me, you send for me," Coco said.

Buchanan and Tomás went back into the street. Buchanan still wore the poncho, the sombrero, and still shuffled like a bent old man. There were patrols, some with badges issued by the police. When they were stopped, Tomás, known to work for Cucamongo, was passed on without attention being paid to the figure beside him.

Mayor Castellano dwelt in a fine house on Alvarado Street. Tomás yanked a bell pull, and an irate servant finally answered. Tomás spoke to him in peremptory

Spanish. The man resisted for a moment, then retreated. Buchanan admired the bellboy from the hotel more and more. Working undercover had given him strength and ability.

Castellano appeared, wrapped in a woolen robe, his feet in slippers, his long hair only half-brushed. "Tomás! This is an unseemly hour."

"To meet Señor Buchanan?"

Castellano stepped back and bade them enter. Buchanan towered over him, straightening, doffing the sombrero. The little man was straight-backed, his chin was hard and proud, his eyes intelligent and sparkling.

"Ah, yes. Buchanan. You have returned."

"Uh-huh. But I won't last long if somethin' isn't done."

Tomás added, "They are patrolling. You know them, sir. They would throw him in their jail. They would beat him, at the very least. They might even, if pressed, kill him and pretend he was being rescued by our people, or escaping. Any excuse to get rid of him and blacken his name."

"I understand. And your suggestion is?"

"A trial. Right now. Tonight. In the theater. A great show. I have already alerted our people. Cucamongo cannot refuse if Judge Carroll calls an emergency trial," said Tomás.

"Impossible!"

"You can do it. Maybe illegal, but you can do it."

"It is ridiculous. It will make fools of us all."

Buchanan said, "Maybe. On t'other hand, your name will be on the tongue of every livin' soul in the West."

Castellano became thoughtful. "True."

Tomás said, "I suggest, sir, you act as prosecutor."

"Prosecutor? Unquestionably you are mad!" cried the mayor.

"Better a friendly prosecutor, sir," said Tomás quietly. "Buchanan will defend himself. If we tell Judge Carroll and Big Jim that Buchanan will appear, there should be no trouble."

"It is madness."

"We can gather possibly fifty guns," Tomás went on, his voice rising a bit. "People who have lived under the oppression of Cucamongo's bribed officials. Your enemies and mine. We will maintain order. There is a newspaperman here, the veteran Dan DeQuille, staying at the hotel. The story will go across the country, possibly even to Europe. To Spain!"

Castellano seemed to grow in stature. "To Spain!"

Tomás said, "I will see that Judge Carroll is informed."

"I'll take care of Cucamongo," Buchanan offered.

"You will be killed!"

"I think not, if we act fast."

Tomás said in a low voice, "Sir, I have waited long. I have worked as a menial. I have been sworn at by filthy but rich gringos, kicked by Cucamongo before I learned my job. Now is our time. We must act."

Castellano looked at Buchanan, who nodded.

"I speak your language," he said. "I savvy what the boy is saying. Cucamongo can turn Los Angeles into a whorehouse and gambling hall. He'll do it, too."

Castellano said, "The theater—his theater."

"On stage. With the footlights burning," whispered Tomás. "A brilliant scene. You are a lawyer, sir. You can appreciate."

"Yes. I can appreciate." Castellano strutted. Then he smiled. "If the profession of actor was respectable . . . Ah, me. I shall be there!"

They departed hastily, lest the volatile mayor change his mind. Buchanan resumed his slouching disguise, Tomás walked briskly.

"How you goin' to handle Judge Carroll?" asked Buchanan.

"Around the hotel one learns things. He has a mistress.

He also has a stern wife whom he fears, and a young daughter. Also—he can be made to believe it is a chance to hang you. Judge Carroll is not brilliant."

Buchanan said, "Cucamongo is smart. But not that smart, I don't believe. It's Hatfield. He's very smart so long as he is on the hunt, the chase."

"Get Cucamongo and Hatfield is nothing."

"Yeah. We'll work on that. The theater, then. Can you send word to Coco?"

"Indeed. And good luck, amigo." The jaunty young man swung away. He was the actor, Buchanan thought. He played the part well enough to fool anyone, the bellhop lurking behind the palm, his hand out for tips . . . and all the while listening and learning and weaving his web throughout the city.

He came to the alley between the hotel and the theater. He listened. There were footsteps, heavy, measured. When they came close, Buchanan jumped around the corner fast as light. He came face to face with Chino Cruz, crouching.

"Out of here, bum," said the prizefighter. "Not allowed."

"How you do go on," Buchanan said. He hit Chino in the belly with a left, then threw a hard uppercut to the neck. Then he kicked the big man's feet from under him. He bent and found the dark lantern and a revolver, which he appropriated.

Chino croaked, "Buchanan. You will die here. You will die, I tell you."

"Uh-huh. Me and a few others, unless you behave. Now get up and walk."

Chino arose, somewhat bent in the middle. He walked to the door of Cucamongo's office. He knocked and spoke as Buchanan ordered, flinching from the gun at his ear. He went in ahead, shielding Buchanan until the door was closed behind them. Then he drew back, against the wall, still breathing hard.

Cucamongo was seated at his desk, a glass of whiskey at his elbow. The top drawer was open, and he reached for it. Buchanan stepped in and swung a hard hand. Cucamongo's head swiveled, he almost fell from the chair.

Buchanan removed the revolver from the drawer. "Kinda lost your head, didn't you? Want me hanged, don't you?"

"You bastard," said Cucamongo. There was a streak of red running from his nose. He wiped it and looked at his hand in pure disbelief. "You're hangman's meat right now."

"Hatfield and the boys out lookin' for me?" Buchanan laughed. "Wastin' their time. There's to be a trial, Big Jim. Tonight. In your theater whether you like it or not. Afterwards, could be you'll be Little Jim."

"A trial? You're crazy, Buchanan." He dabbed at his nose with a kerchief.

"It's my neck," Buchanan pointed out. "Bring all your fine-feathered friends. The mayor will be there, and a jury will be brought in. Not your jury, I'm afraid, but one that'll listen to evidence and believe whichever side they think is right."

"So you want to hang? It's suicide, is it? What happened to the woman you brought cross-country? She turn you down?"

Buchanan slapped him again. This time Cucamongo spun the other way under the force of the blow.

"See you in court," Buchanan said. He stared down Chino Cruz. "You follow me and I may have to kill you. Savvy?"

Chino had not moved from the wall. Cucamongo was unable to speak, holding the kerchief to his face.

It seemed a satisfying situation as of now. Buchanan departed.

There were many people in the streets now, some hurrying toward the Coliseum Theater. Groups of men yelled at one another, and there were gunshots. Buchanan dodged and ducked as he made his way to the hospital to collect Jenny and the doctor.

When he arrived, he paused to get his breath. He was sweating. He took off the poncho and the big hat and stowed them beneath a flowering bush. He had two extra revolvers that weighted down his jacket. He stood a moment thinking of what might happen and of what had gone before.

He thought of Jenny's last words to him. He thought of the thousand and one things they had shared coming across country the hard way, on the run. She had never been daunted.

He thought of Dr. Farrar, who had twice saved him, once on the operating table and once in aiding him to escape. He remembered the look on the slender young man's face when Jenny had made the remark about people thinking Buchanan was her husband.

He heard a sound coming from the hospital that was not normal. Alarmed, he ran quickly for the back door. There was no young man in a white coat to greet him. The patients slept, making the sounds of the sick. Buchanan ran to the front of the house where the operating room was located.

They had Jenny strapped to the table. Dugan had a sharp knife at her throat. Wilks was laughing, his back to Buchanan. Hatfield was whispering questions for Wilks to relay to Dr. Farrar, who was at bay under their guns.

Buchanan fired one shot. Hatfield stared, whirled, and sped for the front door. Dugan dropped the knife and held his stinging wrist. Wilks went down as Buchanan struck him from behind.

It was not the time to ~~go~~ after Hatfield. Buchanan gathered two more revolvers and emptied them, tossing them into a corner. Dr. Farrar was fumbling at the straps holding Jenny to the operating table.

Buchanan picked up the knife. He thumbed the edge, looking from Dugan to Wilks. "I'm a peaceable man," he said. "But you people and your boss have made me damn mad. Right now you get yourselves over to the theater. Your boss'll be lookin' for you. And if you see Hatfield, give him my regards and tell him Cucamongo'll want him there, too."

They scrambled to get out of the hospital. Neither had uttered a word, both looked scared almost to pieces. Buchanan made a gesture, and they went even faster.

Jenny rubbed her wrists. Then she went into the adjoining office and looked into a mirror, her hands going to her hair. She said, "Buchanan on the spot. He always does it."

"They were trying to learn where you were," said Farrar. "We couldn't have told if we wanted. I must warn you, Hatfield is not quite sane on the subject. He cannot talk, but even without words he conveys his hatred."

"He's a hard man," Buchanan said. "I think we can go to the theater now."

"The theater?"

"For my trial. If Jenny could sorta disguise herself one more time?"

She said, "Why not, indeed?"

Dr. Farrar said, "Thank you, sir. I would have told them something . . . anything. If they did not believe me . . ." He shuddered, pale-faced.

"Forget it," Buchanan advised him. "Think about gettin' us to the theater without bein' seen by Hatfield. He'd kill any of us about now, I reckon. Cucamongo don't mean much to him this time."

"I agree," said Dr. Farrar.

Jenny spoke from the next room. "Will this do?"

She was wearing a bright shawl, and in her hair was a decorative Spanish comb. She had done something to her eyes, and her lips were full and curved and red. She walked toward them, her hips swaying and they saw she was wearing red dancing slippers.

Buchanan said, "Looks like a different gal, all right."

"The good doctor evidently has a Spanish lady friend," she said demurely. "You like the skirt?"

It was very full, and when she swung it her ankles were well exposed. Buchanan clapped his hands. Dr. Farrar flushed.

"A patient," he said hastily. "She was a dancer. She could not pay, so she ran away one night."

Buchanan winked at Jenny. "Pretty good story, Doc. Not great, but pretty good."

"It's the truth," Farrar protested. Jenny had swept to the door, and Buchanan was urging him on. He bit his lip and followed them.

Jenny walked ahead, hips rotating. A patrol paused to stare and whistle. Buchanan slid through shadows while Dr. Farrar, well known to all in the city, took Jenny's arm and sent the men on their way.

"When we get in the theater," Buchanan said. "Keep out of sight if you can. I want to surprise them."

"Yes," said Jenny. "It'll be easy."

"I doubt that," Buchanan replied. "But you'll manage."

His admiration for the woman was tremendous. She was the most capable, cool individual he had ever known. He watched Dr. Farrar hang onto her arm and was slightly envious. He had thought from the beginning that Jenny O'Brien was the last woman in the world for him. Now he was only sure that the good doctor was a far better prospect for her.

Outside the theater, there were people from all walks of life, a cross section of Los Angeles. Despite the lateness of the hour, they seemed alert, concerned. Buchanan led the way around to the back door. Coco was waiting.

"Tomás thought you'd come this way. Everything's okay. They're all in there. Exceptin' Hatfield. He ain't nowhere. Tomás's people looked, couldn't find him."

Buchanan frowned. "I don't like that. I don't like it nohow. He saw me at the hospital and ran. He didn't even take a shot at me."

"He had a backup plan," suggested Dr. Farrar.

"He didn't run because he was scared," Buchanan said.

It was a worriment, but he had to face the present and would need all his faculties sharpened for what was about to take place. They went in the door and to the wings. Jenny vanished into a dressing room. Farrar waited at the door, his hands opening and closing. Buchanan took one of the confiscated revolvers from his pocket, checked it, handed it over. "Might need that. Take care of her."

He removed the poncho and the hat. He shook himself, wearing his vest, his cartridge belt, and Colt. There was a gun in his pants pocket and one in his belt. He felt foolish with all that armament—he seldom wore any. He went from the wings onto the stage and stood where the footlights shone on him, a huge, sandy-haired, freckled figure, whose name already rang in the halls of Western history and tradition.

The auditorium was filled. There was instantaneous applause from some of the audience. Another section hissed and booed. The latter was by far the most numerous. Cucamongo's people had done well in stacking the theater.

Coco said, "They don't like us too much."

The artful and swift organizer Tomás had caused the stage to be well set. A throne from *King Lear* was center; the jury box, now being filled by citizens of varying hues and outward apparel—chosen by Tomás and Cucamongo in turn, it seemed—was made of pews from a church scene in a forgotten melodrama. There was a chair for the witnesses. Mayor Castellano, dressed soberly in black and white, was shuffling papers at a small table. Dugan and Wilks, bruised, were in the background. The backdrop behind which they had lurked on the night of the prize fight was raised. Tomás forgot nothing, Buchanan thought.

The jury box was filled. The audience moved restlessly. Then Judge Carroll walked from the wings across from Buchanan, wearing a black robe, a small rascal suddenly endowed with the majesty of the law. Someone called, "Everybody stand," and they did so, including those in the theater audience.

Judge Carroll took the throne of King Lear and said in a somewhat squeaky voice, "This court is convened."

They were all present but Hatfield. It occurred to Buchanan that he might well clear his name in this weird night court—and lose his life. Hatfield would be gathering forces, the "lawmen" deputized by him and paid by Cucamongo. Which way they would come was the problem.

He whispered to Coco, "Watch this side of the house. If you see Hatfield or anything to do with him, yell."

"Guns again?" Coco made a face.

"Could be guns. Could be anything. Whatever, it'll be bad medicine, and you know it."

"I'll keep an eye peeled. I see that Chino over yonder with Dugan and Wilks. I'll watch him, too."

Buchanan could not resist saying, "Why, he's easy. Two punches will take care of him . . . *without* someone hitting him in the head with a club."

Coco said fiercely, "Okay, Tom. Okay. After all this is over, it's you and me. Some place, sometime, I'm gonna learn you!"

Castellano was advancing to the bench presided over by Carroll. He beckoned to Buchanan to join him. A lean, elderly man lounged up the steps leading to the stage, a wad of copy paper in his hand. He winked at Buchanan. It was the man known as "Dan DeQuille," originally and forever a Virginia City newspaper reporter, now nationally known and acclaimed. He found a prop chair and sat down, ignoring the judge and all else, tilting his head, crossing his knees. The story of the trial under his by-line would go all over the world indeed, Buchanan knew.

Judge Carroll was saying, "Buchanan, you understand you are herewith charged with murder in the first degree?"

"Uh-huh," said he. "I mean, I do, sir."

"And Mayor Castellano, you are the prosecutor?"

"I am . . . sir."

"And you, Buchanan, intend defending yourself, although conviction means that you will hang by the neck until you are dead?"

"I do," said Buchanan.

"The prosecution will begin," said the judge.

Castellano looked at the notes he held. "I call Preston Jerome Hatfield."

The judge repeated the name in a loud voice. There was no response. Cucamongo growled, but nobody heeded him.

Castellano said, "If the witness is not present, I will call . . . James Cucamongo."

The mayor wasn't wasting any time, Buchanan decided. This was a tight spot, all those people in the audience, preponderantly unfavorable. Castellano wanted to get it over with as soon as possible before tempers could run short.

Tomás was playing court clerk, holding a prop Bible from one of the dressing rooms. He was also wearing a long-barreled Colt revolver. Cucamongo glared at him, unbelieving. Tomás indicated the Bible, sneering just a trifle. Cucamongo gulped down his outrage and took the oath.

Castellano became meticulous, following legal procedure, identifying Cucamongo as a citizen and a property owner and a "friendly witness" for the state. Cucamongo, suspicious from before the start, answered cautiously, his eyes often wandering. Looking for Hatfield, Buchanan surmised.

They were both waiting for Hatfield. The man's absence was far more cogent than his presence would be. Buchanan scanned the premises, trying to foresee what kind of attack might be initiated.

Cucamongo was spinning his tale, a web of lies about what a good friend to O'Brien he had been, how Buchanan had quarreled with O'Brien, how the murder had been accomplished, from behind. Several times, Castellano looked his way, motioning to him. He could have objected to much of the testimony, he supposed. He was not interested. He wanted them to tell their stories, all of them, knowing they would exaggerate. He had been in many a court in his time—although never as a defendant in a murder case—and had come to his own conclusions about the transaction; he considered it dull and tedious business, clumsily presented. And outside in the night there was Hatfield.

Up above there were the flies, that is, the high parallels from which the backdrops for stage productions were hung. Buchanan stared at them for a long time.

Behind him was the hallway, off which were the dressing rooms. He could see Dr. Farrar standing guard. Beyond was the door through which they had entered the theater. There was no other back door that Buchanan knew about—but there were windows at the other side of the stage.

There was also the front entrance to the theater proper. It was dark out there, only a couple of wall-lamps flickering. A man, several men, could walk in and slip down the aisles. Or they could command the stage from the back of the house with rifles. Everybody on stage would be a well-lighted target. He brooded, wondering, knowing the attack would come.

Castellano said loudly, pointedly, "I have no more questions of this witness."

Judge Carroll asked, "Cross-examine?" as if he hoped Buchanan would refuse.

"Uh-huh," said Buchanan. He whispered to Coco, "Get Jenny ready."

He went to where Cucamongo sat. He cocked his head to one side and asked mildly, "You saw me backshoot Peter O'Brien?"

"I did." He smirked. "I got your gun in my safe. Two shots fired out of it. I got witnesses . . ."

"Objection," drawled Buchanan. "He's the witness."

"Sustained," grunted Carroll, watching DeQuille and his busy pencil, clearing his throat, shaking his head at Cucamongo. The little judge was playing it cagey. He dared not go out too far on a limb. He would favor Cucamongo—but he would protect himself.

Buchanan said, "Okay, Now, who else was present when O'Brien was killed?"

"Law officers," said Cucamongo righteously. "Dugan, Wilks, and Hatfield. They'll tell what happened, just as I said."

"No one else?"

"Nobody but you!"

"And who shot me?" demanded Buchanan.

"One of the officers."

"One of the law officers shot me in the back?"

"To prevent you from murdering us all."

"Objection," said Buchanan.

"Sustained. The jury will ignore Mr. Cucamongo's statement," intoned the judge.

"And no one else saw all this?"

"Nobody."

"And you have my gun in your safe? The law doesn't have possession of it?"

"Why, it was just there. I mean—nobody asked me for it."

"I'll want to pick it up later on." Buchanan grinned.

"You'll be hangin' by the neck later on."

Judge Carroll said plaintively, "Now, Mr. Cucamongo, that's not proper talk in court. It's not for you to say. You keep that up and I'll have to hold you in contempt of court."

Cucamongo's stare projected enough contempt to put him into prison for a long term, but he shut his mouth tight.

Buchanan addressed the court. "Your honor, there's no use me askin' questions of this witness. He's a liar."

"Now you are out of order!" cried the judge.

"Uh-huh. I apologize. Well, the rest of his crew might's well testify. Then I got one witness. Just one."

"Mr. Castellano," said Carroll. "You may proceed."

Castellano called Dugan and Wilks. Both talked too much, protested too much, Buchanan thought. He sensed uneasiness and impatience out in the theater, where decent citizens sat across from blackguards. He asked only one question of each witness, "And no one else saw the killing, the shooting?" All denied that anyone else had been present.

Buchanan subsided. Hatfield would be moving in. He would not be alone. If there was an acquittal, Hatfield would attack in a way to go undetected. Open murder was out of the question—in fact, it would be unnecessary if Buchanan were condemned to be hanged. But Hatfield wanted personal revenge, Buchanan was absolutely certain of that.

He said, "I call Jenny O'Brien to the stand."

Now there was indeed a stir among the people in the theater. The jurors shifted in their chairs, leaning toward one another, whispering. Judge Carroll hammered for order. Dr. Farrar and Coco remained in the wings. Jenny walked onto the stage, into the lights.

She was demure as a country maiden now. Gone was the color from her lips, her hair was braided and coiled tightly to her skull. Her cheeks were pale. The skirt no longer swirled, she walked with short, constrained steps. She seemed frail, helpless. She appealed to them all with a soft glance. She timidly took the oath, looked for the chair, and seated herself with knees tight together and hands folded in her lap.

Cucamongo sat rigid with anger and surprise. Dugan and Wilks spoke in his ear. He shrugged but bit his lip as Buchanan gave him a long, hard, confident, cold look and then began his questioning.

He established her relationship to Peter, asked about her late husband, Peter's brother.

"He was shot and killed in a gambling game with Mr. Cucamongo," she said. Her voice was low, but it projected to every corner of the hall.

"That's out of order, got nothin' to do with this case," said Cucamongo. "I know my rights."

Buchanan addressed the bench. "Your honor, it all relates. Also, the bet made between Mr. Cucamongo and Mr. O'Brien on the prizefight."

"Now, I don't know . . . " The judge broke off, scowling. People were murmuring, the sound was growing. At least half the jurors grumbled.

"Was there such a bet?" Buchanan asked Jenny.

"Yes, sir. There was. Mr. Cucamongo held a mortgage on the ranch after the gambling incident." Her voice was sweet as a flute, she was solemn as an owl. "Peter bet on Coco Bean, bet the ranch against the mortgage."

"A lie," shouted Cucamongo.

"Is it true that after the shooting the mortgage was foreclosed by Mr. Cucamongo?"

"Yes, sir. It's true."

Now the restlessness became so obvious that Judge Carroll threatened everyone with everything, including clearing the theater—the court—which made people laugh. He swallowed hard, and Buchanan lifted a hand. There was quiet in the house.

Buchanan asked, "And where were you when the shooting of Peter O'Brien and myself took place?"

She waited, looking straight at Cucamongo, at the swelling of his neck, the red blood in his fat cheeks. Then she spoke very clearly, her voice rising and falling, all her dramatic training in every syllable.

"Peter O'Brien was killed by Hatfield. Cucamongo ordered Deputy Dugan to shoot Mr. Buchanan in the back. I saw it and heard it all."

Cucamongo was on his feet shouting, "You lie, you wench! There was nobody around but a nun!"

The silence fell, absolute. Judge Carroll shrank into his dapper clothing, his face white as a sheet. Dugan and Wilks, not too bright themselves, realized that an admission had been made by inference, looked for an exit. Castellano motioned to Tomás, who waved to dark-skinned men with shotguns who came out of deep shadows, crouching, waiting.

Jenny said demurely, "Ah yes. I was that nun. In fear of my life because of Cucamongo's threats, I had disguised myself to spy upon him for Peter, and thus I saw what happened."

Carroll pounded for order but the jury was already talking among themselves again and even those who favored Cucamongo were shrugging, spreading their hands. There could be but one result, Buchanan knew.

And he looked for Hatfield. The man had to be somewhere about, someplace from which he could hear what happened, anticipate the verdict if possible. Every moment of the proceedings from now on was fraught with danger for Jenny, himself, and Coco.

Castellano was cross-examining. Cleverly, he was buttressing Jenny's straightforward story merely by encouraging her to talk. Cucamongo held to the seat of his chair with both hands to keep himself from exploding. His cohorts in the theater were uncomfortable, awaiting a leader to bring them to action, perturbed by the frozen condition of Big Jim and his judge on the bench.

Tomás had put down the Bible and was leaning the shotgun against a prop where it would be handy. Castellano was finishing his address to a jury that, everyone knew, would not leave the box without pronouncing the verdict "Not Guilty." Dan DeQuille, an old hand at recognizing mob scenes, had already put away his wad of paper and was edging toward the wings and the exit.

Jenny was now standing next to Coco, who was talking to her, abjuring her not to leave him, to wait for Buchanan. Dugan and Wilks were flanking Cucamongo on his chair, the chair he seemed unable to leave.

There would be a holocaust if someone turned loose the Cucamongo people, Buchanan knew. Inside the hall there would be blood and more deaths than need be. Of them all, only Hatfield could do it at this juncture. And Hatfield still held back wherever he was.

Dr. Farrar came from the wings and stood with Buchanan, his finely chiseled features calm. He whispered, "May I take her out if the shooting begins in here?"

"Certain," said Buchanan. "Watch her while I talk to the jury over yonder."

He spoke briefly. "I dunno what you're thinkin' among yourselves. But I know the lady, Mrs. O'Brien, told the truth. And I know if I hadn't got away—and brought her back here to talk to you—I'd be dead and buried and forgotten by now. And everybody'd believe us frontier people were ugly and bad, killers for no reason. But you know better'n that. All I ask now is for my name to be cleared before the world."

He stepped back. The judge addressed the twelve good men and true, trying his best to twist words so that they would vote against Buchanan, getting his tongue fuzzy, stammering so that they looked pityingly at him. The foreman leaned to the others in the box and said, "Don't think we need to leave the courtroom, your honor . . ."

Sweat stood out on Buchanan's brow as he tried to put himself in the place of Hatfield, to guess where he would strike. If he had cohorts armed and ready to go to war, he might possibly charge in through the lobby of the theater, believing he could get at Buchanan under protective fire. On the other hand, he had been a law officer. Would he invite slaughter of innocents?

The foreman was now saying, "Your honor, we find Buchanan innocent. We advise holding James Cucamongo for trial along with Hatfield, Dugan, and Wilks, and sundry others who were involved in the murder of Peter O'Brien."

Cucamongo came alive as though struck with a knife blade. He came off the chair as if it were a hot stove-lid, screaming, "This is a goddamn kangaroo court! You can't do this to me in my town!"

Guns were unlimbered; Buchanan jumped to where he could command the whole scene, his Colt sticking out, the other revolver in his hand. Before anyone could let loose with a shot, Tomás's voice rose above the hullabaloo, "People! People to the front!"

The young organizer had planned well. Somehow he had furnished all his followers, Spanish and gringo, with shotguns. The twin barrels of these weapons, so utterly lethal at close quarters, sent brave men to their seats, immobile, as though they were hypnotized.

But Dugan and Wilks had no recourse, not with Cucamongo going for his hideout revolver. Buchanan fired the

Colt, then the smaller weapon. He stepped forward, crouching, still searching the front of the house and the flies above for Hatfield.

Dugan went down. Wilks dropped his gun and cried out as he held his shattered right arm. Cucamongo aimed at Buchanan.

Buchanan shot Cucamongo in the left leg. Then he deliberately fired another bullet into his right leg. He wanted the man down, he wanted him alive for trial.

He spun around. Dr. Farrar was tugging Jenny down the hallway that led to the exit into the alley. Coco was banging at Chino Cruz, who had charged. Chino went down the steps into the audience. Judge Carroll was hiding behind the makeshift bench, shivering in his polished boots.

Tomás men held the crowd at bay.

It would not be in here, then, Buchanan thought. Hatfield had abandoned the sinking ship of Cucamongo and was going it for himself. He was implacable; Buchanan must not be the only man who had escaped the always successful hunter of men. Even now, Dr. Farrar was trying to get Jenny into the alley where the killings had begun.

Buchanan started to run. He shouted above the noise of the mob. Dr. Farrar had his hand on the doorknob. Buchanan flew down the passageway. He heard Coco's voice and knew his friend was pounding along behind him.

He roared, "Jenny! Doc! No, wait!"

But Farrar was panicked lest the woman be hurt. He opened the door. A shot spatted and he fell backward, blood starting from his shoulder.

Jenny dropped to one knee, and Buchanan saw she had the revolver he had given her. She fired once, twice, then Buchanan was upon her, shoving her aside and leaping into the alley.

There were a dozen men, and they had him cold. Hatfield was at their head. There were empty chambers in Buchanan's guns, too many of them.

And Hatfield took time to rasp as best he could with his broken jaw, "Buchanan, you're under arrest!"

Buchanan fired his right-hand gun. Then he fired the left-hand gun. Coco went past him like a hurricane, hurling himself into the posse, knocking them about like tenpins. Hatfield went down, but he held the revolver in both hands, rolling over, aiming.

Buchanan felt the blow once more. His right leg went from under him. He sat down, still shooting.

Hatfield's right eye disappeared as he rolled over one more time. Jenny had come into the alley. She stood now with the gun pointed at the men who already were spooked by the shooting of Buchanan and the buffeting by Coco.

She said cooly, "Gentlemen, the party is over. Big Jim is going to the gallows. You want to go with him?"

They looked at Buchanan, who still held a pistol in each hand. They ducked as Coco kept right on swinging at them; then they broke ranks. They began a hasty retreat down the alley. Only Hatfield remained, a sprawled dead man where Peter O'Brien had died all those months ago.

Dr. Farrar came staggering out of the theater holding a handkerchief to his face. He dropped on one knee to examine Buchanan's wound. Coco watched the last of the posse vanish from view, then came to Jenny.

"Guns," he said. "I can't stand it when the guns begin to shoot."

"Buchanan's hit," she said.

"Oh, sure. He always gets some kind of wound from the guns," said Coco indignantly. "Just because I told him that this time I'd really whup him."

Buchanan was walking with the aid of a finely carved cane presented to him by Mayor Castellano for "service to the great city of Los Angeles."

"Looks more like a mudhole to me," he said, watching the rain, rare for the early season, come down in torrents.

Coco said, "You be able to ride pretty soon. Where you goin' next?"

"The high plain," said Buchanan. "Peace in this world. Among friends."

They were in the hospital, where Dr. Farrar was to apply fresh bandages to the flesh wound. Jenny came in and greeted them. She was wearing a long, flowing gown of crinkly material; her hair was up and proper and her face free of powder or paint.

She said, "The court gave me possession of the ranch. Peter had no heirs."

"It could be a payin' concern," Buchanan told her. "Needs attention and some know-how is all."

"I thought as much." She sat down and looked out at the rain. "I could sell it."

"You could." Buchanan grinned. "You could go back to the stage in New York."

After a brief moment, she said, "Buchanan, sometimes you are a big pain in the neck."

"Uh-huh."

"You saw how far I got in New York."

"Uh-huh."

"You know I thought it out and gave it up while we were galavanting across the country."

"Did you, now?"

She said, "Stop the teasing. . . . Will you take over the ranch and put it on a paying basis?"

"Nope," said Buchanan.

"Why not?"

"Can't sit in one place," he told her kindly. "Got to travel and see friends and look at things. Like sky and water and mountains and deserts. Western country. Been away too long. Any good hired hand can run your ranch. But I reckon you'd stay in the city."

"You think I'm a city person?"

"Uh-huh."

She said, "That's what he said."

"After you're married," Buchanan said, "you can weekend at the ranch, check out your foreman. Doc can help, he's a smart, educated young man."

"Who said I was going to marry him?"

"Jenny, you're a brazen hussy. You ain't even blushin'," Buchanan said.

She went to him and kissed him on the cheek. "We were married, too. We were, for a while. Mr. and Mrs. This and That and the Other Thing."

"Uh-huh," said Buchanan.

Dr. Farrar was coming into the office. Jenny drew back. The doctor bore a scar where the bullet had glanced off his jaw, but he was even more handsome for it, Buchanan thought; it gave him a rakish, hard expression that he needed to conceal his soft kindness.

Coco said, "Fix him up good, Doc. I'll get at him and send him back to you when he's able to put up his mitts and fight with me."

"I'm real scared," said Buchanan. He watched the doctor as he gently and carefully removed the bandages. It was time to move on. Nightshade was getting fat on grain in the hotel stable. Los Angeles was peaceful enough under Mayor Castellano and his new deputy, Tomás. But it was not peace in a setting that Buchanan longed for; he had to go out and commune once more with nature. Peaceable, he repeated—he was a peaceable man.